Mr Bingley's Bride

Mr Bingley's Bride

A Sequel to Jane Austen's
Pride and Prejudice
by

Catherine Bilson

ISBN: 0-9954466-2-5
ISBN-13:   978-0-9954466-2-5

Copyright Notice

Contents

Introduction

Mr Bingley's Bride

Being, A Tale of Miss Jane Bennet and Mr Charles Bingley

I've always liked Jane best. She bore her misery with fortitude and grace, she spoke no ill of anyone, even those who most certainly did her wrong. She's always been seen as the quiet, boring one, and in my opinion sadly neglected by English teachers and victimised at the pen of fanfic writers. But she was no fool, and I'd like to think that Charles Bingley discovered he'd married a woman with hidden depths.

   Catherine Bilson, 2017

To Touch An Angel

Jane was quite sure that her cheeks couldn't possibly get any redder. Her one consolation was that her dearest Lizzy sat beside her, companion in her suffering with her hand clasping Jane's tight, her face equally scarlet with mortification.

"And I tell you, my dears," Mama shrilled, waving her hands excitedly, "the first time at least will be quite painful and really very unpleasant. You must merely lie very still and hope that it will be over quickly. With time things become easier, but it is always best, I say, to encourage your husband not to indulge in strong drink if you suspect he might wish to come to your bed, for that will only prolong the experience!"

"I do not think that Mr Darcy cares for strong drink," Lizzy was brave enough to venture after a few moments in which Mama seemed to be gathering her thoughts.

"Then you must be grateful for it! And another thing, do not permit your husband to come to your bed often! Men appreciate much more what they do not get regularly!"

Jane tried not to sigh. Mama was repeating herself now. *Dear God, please let this embarrassing, awful discussion – harangue, rather – be over soo*n. Her wedding on the morrow was something to which Jane had rather been looking forward, until this moment. But now a tight knot of fearful trepidation twisted in her stomach. She gripped Elizabeth's hand tighter, and was comforted a little by the squeeze Lizzy offered in return.

"Mama! Mama!" It was Kitty's voice, and Jane let out a small sigh of relief as her younger sister barged into the room. "You must come! Cook says that the three brace of pheasant you ordered are too high and you must decide what she shall cook instead!"

"Oh, that foolish gamekeeper!" Mrs Bennet stormed from the room and Jane released a larger sigh, along with Elizabeth's hand.

"Thank God that is over!" Elizabeth jumped to her feet. "I am determined that she shall not catch me like that again! How perfectly dreadful!" Turning about, she caught Jane's eye. "Why, Jane, you are as white as a sheet. Do not heed Mama, you know how she exaggerates."

"Lydia said that it hurt the first time too," Jane said rather miserably. "You know I cannot bear pain, Lizzy!"

"Oh, Jane, Lydia was sharing her marriage bed with Wickham, an inconsiderate cad if ever there was one! Aunt Gardiner told me quite different, that if you love your husband and he you, that you need only caution him to be gentle and it may all be quite pleasant, even the first time."

Jane nibbled on her lower lip. "Of course I do love Mr Bingley," she murmured. Elizabeth only rolled her eyes expressively.

"And he loves you to perfect distraction." Eyeing Jane's face, Elizabeth paused, and then enquired "He *has* kissed you, has he not?"

"Lizzy!" Jane's face flamed. "Of course not!"

"Really?"

"Have you been letting Mr Darcy kiss you?" Jane was quite shocked.

"Once or twice," Lizzy admitted it quite unrepentantly. "It is very pleasant, to be kissed. Jane, I really do think you ought to let Bingley kiss you at least once before the wedding."

"You mean, on the mouth, do you not?" Jane asked hesitantly. "He has kissed my hand quite a few times now, and once he was very forward, he turned my hand over and kissed my palm, when no one could see..."

"Yes, Jane, on the mouth," Lizzy rolled her eyes again. "This afternoon, when he comes to visit with Will."

Jane still could not get over the fact that Elizabeth called the stern Mr Fitzwilliam Darcy *Will*, in such a casual and smiling way, even to his face. Nor could she believe the expression that always came over Darcy's face when she did, a shockingly intimate stare that made Jane quite sure that he had forgotten there was any other person in the world but Elizabeth. Jane was barely used to thinking of Mr Bingley as *Charles* in the privacy of her own mind, and certainly she had never dared to speak his Christian name aloud to his face.

"Jane, you must let him kiss you," Elizabeth interrupted her thoughts. "I will suggest that we all go for a walk in the gardens. Take Bingley into the ramble, you can easily go out of sight of the house there, and I promise that Will and I shall not interrupt." She smirked a little. "I can keep Will busy."

Jane's cheeks flamed again at the implication, but she was not truly shocked. Elizabeth was so much braver, so much more confident than she. It was perhaps no surprise that she had dared to experiment with Darcy's kisses, though Jane was very confident that Elizabeth had allowed their intimacy to go no further than that.

Elizabeth, taking Jane's silence for acquiescence and desperate to avoid her mother saying anything embarrassing to Darcy this afternoon, suggested the walk as soon as was polite, barely allowing the men time to make their courtesies, and neatly disposing of Mary and Kitty by claiming that she was sure their bridesmaid's dresses might benefit from another riband or two, under Mrs Bennet's supervision. Kitty was most certainly amenable – in her opinion, the dress Lizzy and Jane had asked her to wear was abominably plain – but Mary's protestations were such that Mrs Bennet's attentions were fully engaged.

Jane could not help but notice how dashing Mr Bingley looked that fine afternoon. His curly fair hair gleamed under the afternoon sun: he chose to leave his hat off as he offered her his arm and led her out through Longbourn's front entrance. He was a good deal taller than she; Jane had to tilt her head up to meet his eyes as he asked her where she would like to walk.

"Perhaps into the ramble?" Jane said shyly. "I do not care to walk far today. It is hot and I do not wish to become tired. I –– I am quite nervous, I own, and I fear I will not sleep well tonight."

For a few moments, Charles did not speak, merely watching as Darcy and Elizabeth turned away and walked down the lane. He led Jane under the rose arch at the entrance to the ramble. "You are nervous, Jane?"

"Well, I suppose I am, a little," she cast a peek up at him under the brim of her bonnet. "It is, after all, not every day that a girl is to be married." When he did not speak for a moment, she asked in a small voice: "Are you not nervous too... Charles?"

He startled, obviously as aware as she that it was the first time she had ever dared to address him by his given name. "I own I am not nervous at all," he said finally, drawing to a stop beside the giant beech tree near the centre of the ramble. The tree was so old and massive that the five Bennet sisters together, standing fingertip to fingertip, had just been able to reach all around it. With the tree between them and the house, Jane was suddenly acutely aware that she and Charles were very much alone. "I am, though, quite *excited*."

"Oh," Jane gulped as Charles put a gentle finger beneath her chin and lifted her face so that she must look at him.

"I have loved you and wanted you for my own since the moment I first laid eyes upon you," Charles said, his blue eyes fixed upon her face. "I could not be happier that the day is finally upon us, but Jane, my sweet angel – I do not want you to be nervous."

She could not speak. There seemed to be a lump the size of her fist blocking her throat.

"Don't be afraid of me, Jane," he said, his voice deeper and softer than she had ever heard it, and then he was leaning down, tilting his head to avoid bumping it on the brim of her bonnet, his warm, soft lips brushing hers for a brief instant.

"Was that it?" Jane blurted out a moment later, and then clapped a hand to her mouth in horror at her own forwardness.

Fortunately, Charles laughed. "Your first kiss a little disappointing, my dearest love? I didn't want to frighten you – but pray allow me to make amends." Gently he plucked her hand from her mouth, and replaced it with his lips.

The second kiss was much more satisfying. And much more dangerous, Jane dimly registered, little thrills of pleasure coursing up and down her body as Charles drew her gently into his arms and kissed her most thoroughly. His tongue even parted her lips and gently caressed her mouth. For a moment her hands fluttered uncertainly, and then she settled them cautiously on his shoulders, feeling with pleasure strong muscles shifting as his arms tightened around her waist.

Charles' breathing was ragged when he finally ended the kiss. "Oh Jane, my own, my sweet angel," he pressed his cheek to hers, his arms still holding her close. "Don't be angry with me."

"Angry with you?" Jane could hardly find her voice. "Why should I be angry with you?"

He laughed then, and moved back a little, taking her small hands in his large, strong ones. "I thought that perhaps my kisses were a little too, *enthusiastic*."

"Oh!" Scarlet-cheeked, Jane cast her eyes down, and then she peeked up at him through long lashes and whispered; "I liked it." To her absolute astonishment she was then the recipient of a look as heated as any she had ever seen Darcy give Elizabeth. Charles' eyes hooded and darkened, and he drew in a sharp breath.

"Don't fear the morrow, Jane," Charles said after a moment, when he regained control over his voice. "I know not what nonsense your mother has filled your head with, but I would beg that you only trust in me. I love you and I swear I will never hurt you."

Jane flushed prettily and cast her eyes down again, but she tucked her little hand into the crook of his arm and almost leaned against him. Charles battled down the fierce arousal he had felt in her presence since the very first moment, cursing both the current fashion for tight breeches and high-waisted coats and Jane's propensity for looking down shyly. He only hoped that she was innocent enough not to realise how aroused he was. She had no brothers, which was a great comfort to him at that moment!

Charles admired Jane unabashedly as she walked beside him. God, but she was beautiful: quite the most handsome woman he had ever met. No Diamond of the *Ton* could hold a candle to her in his estimation. Her blonde hair was the colour of ripe wheat, softly curling around her beautiful cheeks. He longed to see it down, wondering how long it was; at least halfway down her back, he suspected from the thickness of the coils at her nape, maybe more.

Jane peeked shyly up at him once more and began, as was her wont, to politely fill in the silence. She was so sweet, so gracious in all things; she even put up with his impossible snob of a sister with not a hint of annoyance. Charles lost himself in her eyes, a shade he could not quite describe, somewhere between blue and green, a light aqua that he had never seen on anyone else. Such pretty eyes, and there was no featherbrain behind them, he was sure, for he had heard her converse knowledgeably on many subjects. Not that she ever started intellectual conversations, she was too shy for that, but she always listened intently and if pressed to respond would say something that clearly indicated a comprehension of the subject.

Charles knew that both Jane and Elizabeth often availed themselves of their father's library as the only place of respite in Longbourn from their mother and sisters' nonsense, but it was evident to him that they did not waste their time with novels. Jane had indeed responded to a subtle put-down from Caroline, when Caroline had spouted off a few words in Italian, Jane had responded in far more

21

fluent terms and a perfect accent. When he asked her about it later, she had murmured something about a small gift for languages.

No, Jane Bennet was no dumb blonde, unlike her idiotic youngest sister and her silly, fluttering mother. The other two sisters Charles reckoned salvageable: Mary was bright enough if not too pretty, and Catherine was pretty if not all that bright. She was at least bright enough to recognise that modelling her behaviour after that of her older sisters was by far the wisest course left to her after Lydia's reckless madness. Darcy had even murmured something about having his cousin Colonel Fitzwilliam introduced to Kitty at the wedding, though Charles suspected that was just Darcy having a joke on his cousin, for the colonel unfortunately needed to marry well.

Thank God Charles was in the fortunate position of being able to choose his own bride, with no powerful relations to disapprove his choice! Caroline was bad enough, with her barbed comments and sideways glances. At least Louisa was no longer aiding and abetting her, since

Charles' not at all subtle hint to Mr Hurst that perhaps he and his wife would feel more comfortable in Town if Louisa found local society so unbearable. Forced with the prospect of having to live within his own meagre means, Hurst had called Louisa sharply to heel and she had not so much as said boo to a goose since.

Caroline, though, he would have to make mind, Charles knew, and *before* the wedding. He would not have his Jane made uncomfortable for so much as a moment once she was mistress of Netherfield, and he well knew that Caroline would hand over her duties as mistress of his household both grudgingly and with maximum condescension. No, he would not subject Jane to that. Tonight he would steel himself for an undoubtedly uncomfortable, but entirely necessary, private conversation with his sister.

Voices from the lane reminded Charles that Darcy would be returning with Elizabeth. They were not staying to dine with the Bennets tonight – Darcy had said bluntly that tonight was as unbearable as Mrs Bennet was likely to get and begged

Charles quite unashamedly to spare him that.

"Darcy and Elizabeth are returning," he said softly to Jane, who seemed to have fallen into a dreamy kind of reverie. She startled slightly, looked up at him, and blushed, seeming to focus on his lips. Charles could not help but smile, wondering if she had been recollecting that spectacular kiss, and then he just had to bend his head and quickly snatch another.

And so it was that Jane was scarlet-cheeked and giggling as Elizabeth entered under the rose arch and saw her. Elizabeth laughed herself and came to take her favourite sister's arm.

"Why, Mr Bingley, I dare not ask what you have said to Jane to make her blush so!" she said archly.

"I have not *said* anything," Charles protested with absolute innocence, which truthful remark only made Jane blush harder and Lizzy begin to snicker behind her hand.

Charles took his leave of Jane in the drawing-room, with a regretful kiss to her hand and a hidden caress on the inside of her wrist that made her blush again, though she met his eyes with a surprisingly bold stare. He could only think that tomorrow could not possibly come soon enough as he and Darcy departed.

Laying Down The Law

Collecting their horses, Bingley and Darcy set off back to Netherfield at a leisurely pace, neither of them in any hurry to leave behind pleasant memories of the afternoon.

"Miss Bennet looked well today," Darcy said politely after a little while, and Charles smiled. Elizabeth was certainly having a good effect on Darcy: previously he had never felt the need to politely start a conversation.

"She is well," Charles said. "She had some little nerves about tomorrow but I made an effort to reassure her."

"Naturally," Darcy said with a slight smile. "Mrs Bennet has been filling their heads with nonsense, I am sure: Lizzy seemed suddenly to have some small reservations that I needed to overcome."

"It must be unnerving for a young lady, on the eve of their wedding," Charles said reflectively. "Girls are kept so sheltered, so unaware of men; society requires purity in mind as well as body, does it not? And then suddenly, without foreknowledge, they are expected to surrender all in an act so intimate even their mothers cannot seem to bring themselves to discuss it rationally!"

Darcy grinned slightly, and then frowned, no doubt thinking of his sister.

"Though Georgiana is fortunate, Darce: when the time comes she will have Elizabeth to explain things to her, and I do not think Elizabeth will be so missish as to frighten her."

"I'll thank you not to mention it! It will be a good many years if ever before I allow Georgy to wed!"

Charles laughed at Darcy's expression and turned his horse toward the track that would lead them to Netherfield. "I don't think you'd ever consider there to be a man worthy of little Georgy!"

Darcy shook his head in agreement. "Sisters are the very devil!"

That only made Charles grimace, thinking of the necessary conversation to come with Caroline. He did not expect that it would go well.

*　　*　　*

After dinner, when the men had rejoined the ladies in the parlour, Charles approached Caroline and asked if she would attend him in his study as he had some private matters to discuss with her.

"Why Charles, I am sure there is nothing you can have to say to me that the others cannot hear," Caroline said archly, but Charles shook his head very firmly. Several other guests had arrived for the weddings on the morrow, and while he was angered with his sister's behaviour he would not subject her to ridicule and scorn from them by reproaching her publicly.

"In the study, now, if you please, sister."

"Well, pray allow me to take leave of our guests," she said with an affected sigh, but it was a full hour later before she walked into his study without even a courtesy tap on the door.

Charles looked up from a book he had placed on his desk. "Sit down, please, Caroline," he gestured to the chair opposite his desk. Caroline gave him a strange look.

"I think I should be more comfortable here, than in your steward's chair, Charles," she gestured to one of the two comfortable wing chairs by the window, and began to walk in that direction.

"Caroline, you will sit down," Charles made his voice come out sharp and hard, and watched her stop in surprise. She turned to face him, and he pointed again at the chair where his steward sat while taking his direction. "This is not a nice little chat between brother and sister. I am giving you directions which you *will* follow, and as such this is an entirely appropriate seat for you."

Caroline blinked in astonishment. In all of his life she had never heard Charles sound as he did now. She surveyed him and asked "Charles, have you been drinking?"

"Caroline, I am entirely sober, and you will *sit down now*."

She sat, her eyes wide. "I must say that I do not appreciate your speaking to me in this tone..."

"Am I or am I not the head of this family?" he asked her sharply.

"Well yes, of course..."

"And as such, dear sister, I have had quite enough of your questioning my decisions. On the morrow I am marrying Miss Bennet, the love of my life. From this day forward, every disparaging comment you make, every sneer directed in her direction, every subtle put-down upon her origins, will cost you five pounds a month from your allowance. Every. Single. Time."

Caroline sat with her mouth open staring at him in astonishment, no doubt thinking that he had never spoken to her so sharply in his entire life. After a few moments she seemed to collect her thoughts and spoke, her tone conciliating. "But dear brother, you must know I have only ever wanted the best for you!"

"Miss Bennet *is* the best for me, Caroline. I have made it very clear on many occasions that I admire her above all women in England. Your implication that she is not is yet *another* put-down to her, and as such your allowance for next month is now down to twenty pounds."

Caroline swallowed the obvious mouthful of retorts that had been about to spew forth and simply sat, slowly turning a very unattractive shade of purple.

"I have already asked you only to speak well of Miss Bennet," Charles said after a few moments. "You did not seem inclined to obey me when I asked you nicely. Apparently money does talk, however. And remember, should you desire me to loose the reins on your inheritance, all you need do is marry! You've had your chances, Caroline: I strongly suggest that if you do not wish to remain in my household that all you need do is accept one of the numerous offers that have been made to you and no doubt will be made again on our return to London."

"Pah!" Offered a new target for her venom, Caroline regained her voice. "Even you, Charles, cannot force me to marry a man I do not want!"

"Perhaps it might be wiser for you to reconsider some of those offers in a new light, now that the man you do want is being removed from the marriage mart," Charles said, not unkindly, but Caroline took it badly.

"I collect you mean Mr Darcy?" she enquired in frigid tones.

"Caroline, do not make any more of a fool of yourself than you already have. You chased him and he chose Miss Elizabeth."

"Scheming little..."

"I do believe that my prohibition on speaking ill of Miss Bennet shall extend to her sister," Charles said before she got any further, and Caroline snapped her mouth shut, though her snapping eyes and high colour expressed her rage.

"Caroline, I will not live with you mistreating my wife," he said it softly but very clearly. "You shall not condescend to her, you shall not malign her – to *anyone* – and you shall treat her as though you are absolutely overjoyed to have Jane as your sister. Because my loyalty will always be to my wife, and I will always take her side from this moment on, I give you fair warning to make your peace with my choice now, or leave my household as soon as you may. You have many friends who are always willing to welcome you into their homes."

Caroline sat rigid, her mouth a tight, unattractive line, and Charles sighed again, wondering if he was going to be saddled with her for the rest of his life. How on earth did he end up with such a social-climbing snob for a sister? He blamed that blasted finishing school in Bath their stepmother had insisted on sending her to.

Louisa was already out and wed by the time their father had remarried, but Caroline was only seventeen and the new Mrs Bingley had deemed that she needed some polish before going out into Society. Charles considered himself lucky to have escaped his stepmother's machinations: he was already at the end of his first year of Cambridge where he had been lucky enough to find Darcy as a friend, a friend of whom his socially-climbing stepmother had most heartily approved.

Charles had every sympathy for the Misses Bennet, for he knew exactly what it was like to have a pushy mother determined to elevate the family's social standing at whatever cost. His stepmother was the one, he was sure, who had encouraged Caroline to catch Darcy. Charles only thanked God that Darcy had no interest in his sister whatsoever. While nothing would make Charles happier than to call Darcy his brother, he was much happier that they would be united through the Bennet family.

"Perhaps," he suggested gently, "a visit to Sir John and Lady Forrest might suit you." Their stepmother had remarried barely six months after their father's death, to an extremely wealthy older man knighted for his services to the Crown. Sir John spared his wife nothing, but had no interest in her children. Caroline would get no extra income there: Lady Forrest might lavish a few gifts on her but that would be all.

There was silence for a few moments, and then Caroline inclined her head, very slightly. "Perhaps I shall write to Lady Forrest," was all she said, and Charles knew that was all the acquiescence he would get from her. He had wounded her pride, for certain, but better a few pins in Caroline's puffed-up notions of herself than that she should wound Jane with her condescension!

"I do not wish to hurt you," he said gently, not liking the stiff, frozen expression on her face. "I have only ever wanted to see you happy, Caroline."

She seemed to sort through her thoughts for a moment, and then said "I only ever wanted to be mistress of Pemberley."

There did not seem to be much he could say to that, only "I am afraid that is something that was never in my power to give you."

"No," she responded coolly, and left it at that. When he said no more, after a few moments she stood, smoothing her skirt. "By your leave, Charles, I will return to our guests. My responsibilities as mistress of your household remain until your wife is ready to take them over."

Charles was about to say something snappish and then paused to reconsider. Somehow he doubted that Jane would be quite ready to take over all responsibilities in his household the very day of her wedding! And indeed – perhaps he would not be willing to let her out of his bed for long enough to do so! Instead he said: "Caroline, you are generous. I have been thinking that I would like to take Miss Bennet away on a short honeymoon for a few days, perhaps next week."

She looked at him surprised. "But where should you go?"

Since the idea had at that very moment popped into his head, Charles took a few moments to consider. "Perhaps to Eastbourne," he said then. "We stayed in a very pleasant hotel there the summer before last, do you recall?"

"The Grand," Caroline said unwillingly. "It was very pleasant, yes."

"I shall write to them requesting a suite, and if they respond that one is available, I shall take Miss Bennet – Mrs Bingley – and you will stay here and take care of Netherfield for me, if you will, Caroline, until our return."

She gave him a stare, and then a shallow curtsy. "I am at your disposal, of course, dear brother."

The tone was sarcastic, but really he had no call to say anything. She had, after all, followed his directives. And there would be no one at Netherfield upon whom she could vent her spite when he was gone: Darcy intended to leave with Elizabeth a day or two after the wedding, taking her straight to Pemberley, while his cousin Fitzwilliam would escort Georgiana on a visit to his parents the Earl and Countess of Matlock. Only Mr and Mrs Bennet and their two remaining daughters would be close enough, and Caroline would look very bad if she could not contain her bile against her newest relatives, no matter how much she disliked them.

Charles reached for pen and paper and began a note to the manager of the Grand at Eastbourne, requesting that they advise by return whether a suite would be available for the newly married couple one week hence. He finished it quickly, sealed and franked it, and on his way back to the drawing-room laid it on the salver in the hallway, to go to post in the morning.

On his entry into the room, Charles spotted Georgiana Darcy attempting to quietly edge her way out of the company, and promptly went to her side. She was a sweet girl regularly in need of rescuing in social situations. He had briefly felt a little awkward in her presence once he realised Caroline's plan that they should marry – in furtherance of her pursuit of Darcy, of course, not from any real belief that they might suit.

"Will you dance with me, Miss Darcy, on my last night as a bachelor?" Charles said loudly. "Come, Louisa, let us have a tune!"

"Oh, but I could play…" Georgiana saw a chance to hide behind the pianoforte, but Charles was having none of it.

"Certainly not, Miss Darcy, for if you play everyone will only wish to sit and listen reverently! Louisa will play and I shall dance your slippers bare!"

Georgiana could not help but laugh and take his hands, and a moment later three more couples had joined the dance, Colonel Fitzwilliam one of them with Caroline, to spare Darcy, who as usual when Elizabeth was not present could not be coerced to dance at all.

Catherine Bilson

The Wedding

Jane did not think that she would sleep a wink. She and Elizabeth were sent to bed quite early, though, and they sat brushing each others' hair by the light of a single candle and talking softly so that they might not be discovered.

"So you did let Mr Bingley kiss you," Elizabeth said teasingly, drawing the brush gently over Jane's hair. Jane was glad she was facing away from her sister, so that Elizabeth could not see her scarlet cheeks.

"Yes," she murmured softly, "yes, I did."

"And do you feel a little better now about what will happen tomorrow?" Jane sensed genuine concern in Elizabeth's question.

"Yes, I do," she answered honestly. She still feared the pain, for physical pain was something that Jane was well aware she did not tolerate well. But she was confident that Charles would be gentle with her and do his best not to hurt her, and after all she had

41

never heard of a woman who died of pain on her wedding night!

"Oh, Jane, I shall miss you so!" Elizabeth laid down the brush and hugged her, and Jane hugged her back.

"Oh Lizzy, you shall not have time to miss me! You shall be busy learning to be mistress of a very grand estate, and sister to Miss Darcy, and wife to Mr Darcy! In no time at all we shall be together again, for Mr Bingley has promised that we shall come to Pemberley for Christmas, and even Papa says that he thinks of coming with Mama and Mary and Kitty, which of course means that he shall if you will just ask him sweetly."

Elizabeth laughed, but there were tears in her eyes. "Promise me that you will write very often, my dearest?"

"Lizzy, it is not I who am reckoned a poor correspondent!" Jane chided laughingly.

Elizabeth laughed too then, a little shame-faced. "I promise I shall try harder! And Jane, there is one thing that you must promise me, that you will not let Caroline Bingley bully you."

"I am sure that she would not," Jane replied, though inside she quaked a little. Caroline Bingley could be ferociously intimidating, and Jane did not look forward to their first confrontation. For confrontation there would be. Jane knew herself to be generous to a fault and liable to give in rather than face conflict, but she would be mistress of Netherfield. And one thing that Mrs Bennet had drilled into her eldest daughter, so beautiful and clearly destined to be wife of a wealthy man and mistress of a grand estate, was that once she was in charge, that she must be In Charge. And that she must at the earliest possible opportunity apprise any potential rivals to her authority of that fact.

"I am very sure that she would," Elizabeth responded.

"You leave Caroline Bingley to me," Jane said firmly, "though it is clear you are far luckier in the sister you will gain than I. Georgiana Darcy is the sweetest girl."

"Is she not?" Elizabeth smiled fondly. "I think she is very much like you were at her age, dearest! And when I think what that blackguard Wickham tried to do..."

They both shuddered in unison. "Horrible to say, but I must be glad that Lydia is now Mrs Wickham and not Georgiana," Elizabeth said then. "At least Lydia has enough strength of character to stand up for herself!"

"I hope so," Jane said, feeling suddenly that her feet were cold. She wriggled under the bedclothes, tying the ribbon in the end of the long braid Lizzy had woven into her hair as they talked. "Blow that candle out, Lizzy. We must try to sleep."

Elizabeth sighed. "I am sure I never shall!" But she complied with Jane's request and crawled into bed. They whispered together a little while longer, until eventually Jane sensed Elizabeth was on the edge of sleep, as her responses became slower and less sensible. Jane fell silent and Elizabeth did not speak again.

Jane lay wakeful for a long time, staring out at the stars. She liked to sleep with the drapes a little open so that she could see the night sky, and wondered if Charles would let her. In summer her room was so stuffy. But then all the rooms at Netherfield were huge, and certainly not stuffy. Jane wondered what her room would be like. She was sure that Charles would allow her to redecorate it if she wished: hopefully he had not let Caroline prepare for the new mistress! Jane shuddered slightly, thinking of the shades of oranges and deep pink that Caroline Bingley seemed to favour.

Thinking of what her room would be like led Jane to wonder. Would Charles come to her room? Would his room be adjoining, and would he expect her to come to him? Surely not! And Jane was very sure that she could not, that she would never be able to walk to his bed in only a nightgown or robe. Her knees failed at the very thought! But then she recalled the heated look that Charles had given her after that kiss and she smiled to herself. No, Charles would come to her, and eagerly, she thought. Jane fell asleep at last with a smile on her face, remembering that kiss, the heat and tenderness of Charles' mouth, the strength of his hands as he held her close.

"Are they still abed?" It was Mrs Bennet's shrill scream that woke Jane. "Hill! Hill! Go and wake Jane and Lizzy directly! Oh, my Lord! We shall never be ready!"

Mrs Bennet's fears were unfounded: both girls were ready in plenty of time to mount the carriage with their father and travel to the church, though one would never have known that they were punctual by the panicked look on Charles Bingley's face. Somehow in the night he had convinced himself that he had terrified Jane with his ardour and that she, a pure and perfect virgin, would find herself utterly unable to go through with the wedding. The expression of relief on his face when Jane entered the church on Mr Bennet's arm was comical to behold, though Darcy who would have been the most likely to laugh at him was entirely occupied in looking his fill at Elizabeth.

The two sisters had chosen to wear identical dresses of purest white satin, delicate bands of Brussels lace at the hems and sleeves. Bingley, who had privately expected a mass of frills as chosen by Mrs Bennet, was utterly delighted. Jane's golden hair was piled in a complex coronet of braids threaded by tiny white rosebuds, and it seemed to him that all she needed was a pair of wings and she would be an angel in truth. She walked the aisle towards him, a soft smile on her beautiful face, and he stepped forward as though in a dream state to claim her hand.

"I have never seen you look so beautiful as you do this day," he whispered, and a pretty blush tinted Jane's pale cheeks.

The wedding ceremony was a blur to Charles, who could do little but stare at Jane. She peeked up at him often from those stunning aqua eyes, that blush still colouring her face prettily, but her voice was steady and clear as she carefully repeated her vows. Bingley was sure he stumbled and stuttered like an absolute buffoon, but all he could think about was that in a few short hours he would have Jane to himself at last.

Darcy had ordered his cabriolet brought up from London for the occasion, and after the church ceremony both couples were seated in the open carriage for the ride back to Netherfield. Local children tossed flower petals at them and Charles laughed as they pulled away, taking off his top hat and shaking the petals from it. Jane was giggling too, plucking petals from her lap and tossing them out of the carriage. Darcy and Elizabeth had escaped the worst of it: Jane had been directly in the path of the petal shower and was quite covered in them, petals tumbling from her hair as she moved her head about. A few white petals had fallen on her chest, and Charles found himself staring arrested as they tumbled down inside the neck of her dress.

"Oh, drat," Jane muttered, trying to scrape the petals off her skin. They slid down into the modest neckline of her dress, and she frowned slightly, wondering if she should try to fish them out of her cleavage. No, best not, that would look immodest at best. She glanced up and caught Charles staring at her neckline, and blushed again.

Charles glanced quickly at Darcy and Elizabeth, who seemed utterly wrapped up in each other, and then he leaned over to Jane and murmured, "I would offer to help but I fear that I would not behave very well once I laid my hands upon you."

Jane wondered just how red her skin was getting. Her cheeks felt exceedingly hot. She murmured, "I thank you for your offer, Charles, but I think it would perhaps be best if I ask a maid at Netherfield to assist me."

"If you want to attend your wedding breakfast, I am quite sure that *would* be best," Charles agreed with a grin, because although the words were reproving, the tone was not, and Jane had a little smile curving the corners of her lips. She was so pretty when she blushed, too. He looked forward to seeing her pink-cheeked very often indeed. Perhaps he could instigate blushes by telling her that she had haunted his dreams since their first meeting... but perhaps she would not yet understand the implication that she had behaved much more wantonly in his dreams than she ever would have in real life.

The wedding breakfast seemed interminable. At least Caroline was on her best behaviour, Charles thought, watching her make polite conversation with the Countess of Matlock and Miss Darcy, undoubtedly the only two women in the room who she did not consider to be most definitely her social inferiors. He looked further across the room and saw Jane, being warmly embraced by her father. If Caroline had been the unhappiest woman at the wedding, Mr Bennet had certainly been the unhappiest man: he very obviously did not like losing his two favourite daughters both at once, and it was evidently a bitter blow that Elizabeth should be moving so far away.

It seemed to Charles to be nearing midnight by the time he was able to bid farewell to his last guests. Darcy and Elizabeth had quite shockingly disappeared a full hour ago, though everyone was too well-mannered to comment, even Mrs Bennet. Jane had never faltered; gracious and charming to everyone, she looked like a slender white rose as she stood at the foot of the stairs, awaiting him. Bingley walked slowly towards her, and when he reached her, lifted her slender hand and brought it to his lips.

"You must be weary beyond belief, Mrs Bingley," he said softly, regretfully revising his plans for the night. "Your new maid Helena will have drawn you a bath: I pray you will enjoy it and then sleep well."

A scarlet blush came to Jane's face, and she thought in sudden panicked misery that he did not want her. But then she realised, *of course not.* It was just Charles being typically generous and considerate. Well, she would have none of that. She had not nerved herself to get through this night, only to have to build her courage up again tomorrow!

"Charles," she said, making herself meet his eyes bravely, "Lizzy and I have always shared a room. I fear I will not sleep well at all if I must sleep alone."

"I do not think that Elizabeth is likely to be available..." Charles began, and then stopped in confusion, feeling like an utter fool as her soft lips quirked in amusement and he realised he had mistaken her meaning. "Oh," he said, quite inadequately.

"Of course, I am sure that you must be tired too," Jane said kindly, "and perhaps my snoring will keep you awake..."

"Somehow I doubt that you snore," Charles said, seeing the glint of humour in her eyes.

"Perhaps not. Lizzy assures me that I kick abominably, though..."

"I shall ask Mrs Darcy, but I suspect you have just told me a falsehood."

"Perhaps you should investigate for yourself, in half an hour or so," Jane said archly. And then she slipped her hand from her husband's and walked away up the stairs, glancing over her shoulder and seeing him grinning at her. Her cheeks had never been so red, she was sure.

Charles could not help but smile. Jane was obviously embarrassed by her own forwardness, but it was equally obvious that she had just issued him with a blatant invitation. One he had no intention of turning down. He waited a few moments and then followed Jane up the stairs, heading for his own room.

It Is No Duty

Jane was delighted with Helena, a pleasant young girl from Meryton who had been specially hired to be her maid. She had an unpleasant suspicion that Caroline had intended to stick her with some old battle-axe, but Charles had actually sent his housekeeper over to Longbourn to consult with Hill about any recommendations she might have for Jane's personal maid, which had delighted Hill no end. Helena was a relative of hers, a very pleasant young girl who had been nicely trained to be a lady's maid. She was quiet and gently efficient as she unlaced Jane's gown and assisted her into the luxurious bath which was set before a roaring fire in her dressing-room. Which was another pleasant surprise to Jane: the rooms which had been prepared for her were lovely, quietly understated but simple, not quite finished, waiting for her hand to turn them into her personal place. She had a dressing-room, a bedroom and a private parlour, a door from which connected to Charles' suite.

Mindful of the time she had allotted Charles, Jane did not allow herself to linger over her bath. Helena dried her and assisted her into her nightgown and wrapper, pretty, lacy things which were a gift from her Aunt Gardiner. The maid was gently brushing out Jane's long hair before her dressing-mirror when there was a quiet knock from the door in the sitting-room.

"That will be all, thank you Helena," Jane said, proud of the fact that she was able to keep her voice calm and steady. The maid bobbed a curtsy and slipped out through the servants' door in the dressing-room as Jane went to answer the door herself.

Her hair was even longer than he had realised, was Charles' first dazed thought. It fell in a thick swirl of golden silk all the way to her hips. Immediately he wanted to fist it in his hands, bury his face in it to inhale deeply of the soft scent of roses that always rose from Jane's skin. He took in every detail of her appearance, of the fine lawn nightgown and wrapper trimmed with delicate Brussels lace, the fact that she was obviously quite unaware of the way the fire behind her silhouetted her lush figure in a way that made him catch his breath.

"You are," he said at last, aware his voice was hoarse with need, "quite astonishingly beautiful."

Jane laughed a little and blushed. She had been gazing at him herself, absorbing his appearance. He seemed taller than ever, and she realised it was because she was barefoot. He wore a dark blue silk robe and loose silk trousers of the same colour, and while the robe was belted, it was open at the collar and she could clearly see the skin of his chest, more heavily muscled than she had thought he would be. Of course he always looked good in his formal clothes, his shoulders broad and strong, but then some men did pad their coats...

Jane's thoughts ran down into incoherency as Charles stepped close enough to take her hands in his.

"Are you quite sure about this, Jane?" he asked her gently. "You must be tired, and we can wait – you need not feel that you must do your duty tonight..."

"I do not think of it as a duty," Jane said honestly. *And I will give your household no cause for gossip if blood should not be found on my sheets in the morn*, she thought to herself. "I want – I want to be truly your wife, Charles," she found words she could make herself utter. "Please."

"Ah, my Jane," he drew her into his arms, pressing his face against the top of her head, and Jane felt absurdly small and fragile beside his strength. "One thing I promise you, and that is that never again will you have to beg me to come to your bed." There was a laugh in his voice, as he drew her gently into her bedroom and over to the great four-poster bed with its subtle cream covers, already turned down deftly by Helena. Jane was too short to sit down on it, though, so with a soft laugh he took her waist in his big hands and lifted her as though she was as light as a feather.

"Oh!" Jane let out a soft gasp as she was lifted off her feet and laid on the thick, soft mattress. And then Charles was lying beside her, his blue eyes gazing into hers as he drew her close. She couldn't help but tense a little, and he smiled at her and shook his head gently.

"Jane, best beloved, relax a little. There is no hurry, and if we rush I'll likely hurt you, and I'd never willingly do that. You need to trust me."

"I do trust you," she whispered, "but Charles, I do not like at all to suffer pain."

"Ah," he smiled ruefully, "I fear I cannot guarantee you that there will be none, not this first time, at least. But I can promise that I will be as gentle and considerate as I can be, and that even if it hurts you this time, that the next time you will find pleasure in lovemaking."

Jane's eyes went wide and surprised, and Charles cursed softly under his breath. What the hell kind of nonsense had her mother been filling her head with, if Jane did not even expect to enjoy her marriage bed?

"Did you like it when I kissed you, Jane?" he asked softly, and watched that pretty blush colour her cheeks again. She nodded mutely. "Then you had best just trust me that you will like the rest a lot better than kissing."

Aqua eyes wide, Jane could only whisper "Could we – could we start with kissing?"

Charles' mouth quirked. "Oh, yes." And he drew her still closer and brought his mouth to meet hers.

Jane's senses reeled under the impact of that explosive kiss, like and yet unlike the way he had kissed her in Longbourn's garden. Perhaps it was that this time Charles was holding nothing back, kissing her with a fierce hunger she sensed he had thus far kept well leashed. And what was most shocking was that his ardour drew an answering, equally passionate response from her of which Jane had never suspected she might be capable. Somehow she found that her hands had worked her way inside the collar of his robe, and she explored curiously his skin, hot and sleek, hard with muscle as his arms shifted to hold her closer.

The gentle, featherlight touch of her fingers on his chest was driving Charles mad. He had to remind himself that this was not the wanton Jane who had inhabited his dreams for many months now, but his

Jane, his real live angel, and that he must not be rough or demanding or he could give her a disgust of his touch that might take a long time to overcome. Gently he tugged on the ribbons of her wrapper, relieved when they came loose at a touch. The neck of her nightgown opened as easily, and he marvelled at the silken softness of her skin. Slowly and gently he trailed his fingers downward, weighing her breast lightly in his hand, brushing the nipple with his palm, feeling with pleasure the way it tightened under his touch.

Jane let out a tiny sound against his mouth, and he stopped kissing her for a moment to ask "Are you all right, my dearest?"

"That feels – shocking, but so nice, Charles," she gasped out, and then a true moan escaped her lips as he tweaked her nipple lightly with his fingertips.

Charles laughed softly. "Jane, you are going to have to suspend your instincts for the night, because I'm going to do a lot more things to you that you will find very shocking indeed if you think too hard about it." He kissed her again, and then began to trail kisses down her throat. "Stop thinking and just let yourself feel, Jane," he ordered, and then his mouth closed lightly over her nipple and he was rewarded by her soft, breathy gasp.

Jane pushed her shock to the back of her mind firmly. She was not going to be missish, she was a married woman now and she would do whatever her husband wished. Her back arched and she could not help but let out a low moan as he nipped her gently. Although she did hope that he would not think that she was too wanton.

"I want – I want to see you," she mumbled, pushing at his shoulders. "Please, Charles – take this off."

He did not hesitate to obey, stripping the robe off one-handed even as he continued his attentions to her breasts. And then one strong hand was wandering lower, pushing her nightgown and robe from her body, stroking lightly over her thighs before settling possessively over her most intimate place.

Jane no longer seemed to have any control over her own body. Charles' strong, yet infinitely gentle hands seemed to be everywhere, exploring where and how she liked to be touched, and she was reacting instinctively, unable to keep from writhing under that gentle, searching touch. Soon his hot mouth was following to her most sensitive spots and she was embarrassed to find that she was moaning incoherently and gasping out his name.

Charles, for his part, was utterly delighted with Jane's responsiveness. Aware that his need for her had built to almost unbearable levels, he was determined that she should have pleasure from his lovemaking before he took her virginity. And so he explored with the greatest delight her body, so lush and soft, that perfect white skin sleeker than the finest silk, loving her more with every tiny sound she made, the flush of arousal suffusing her flesh as finally he moved over her and took her mouth with his. She arched beneath him, begging wordlessly, and he positioned himself carefully and thrust.

The pain was minimal. One sharp pinch, a slightly uncomfortable, heavy, *stretching* sort of feeling deep inside her. And then the pleasure began again, yet more intensely than before, building and building to she knew not what until the world whirled about her and she cried out Charles' name in astonished delight.

"Oh, Jane," he gritted out, feeling silken muscles clench on him, and giving up entirely his battle for control. The climax shook him with its astonishing intensity, and then he collapsed on Jane, groaning her name out again as aftershocks of pleasure rippled up his spine. Her slender arms wrapped around him, and after a moment he realised she was laughing softly.

"Jane?" he lifted his head uncertainly to look at her, and she reached up and kissed him.

"Oh, Charles, that did not hurt at all, and it was so wonderful!" her eyes were starry as she gazed up at him.

"I love you so much," he told her, his heart overflowing even as it still raced with excitement. Her smile was glorious, and no longer shy.

Charles eased from Jane gently, glancing down and grimacing slightly at the sight of the blood smearing her slender thighs. Gently he drew a cover over her. "Wait here," he told her, and in her dressing-room, he dipped a cloth into the cooled bath and wiped himself down quickly, before rinsing it out and returning to tend to his wife. Exhausted and sated, she lay quietly as he washed the blood tenderly from her legs.

"Sleep," Charles whispered, seeing her aqua eyes clouded with fatigue.

"Will you stay with me?" Jane whispered back.

"You could not keep me away," he smiled down at her, and she smiled contentedly and closed her eyes.

Far from kicking him in her sleep, Jane instead curled into his arms like a kitten, rubbing her cheek contentedly on his chest. Charles was sure he had never been so happy in his life, as he closed his own eyes, inhaling the soft scent of roses.

Catherine Bilson

Morning Joy

Jane awoke feeling warm and exceedingly comfortable. She stretched luxuriously, her eyes still closed, and bumped the top of her head.

"Ouch!" she said, just as Charles said the same thing.

"Oh!" Jane's eyes flew open and she realised that she was lying on Charles' chest, and that she had just bumped the top of her head on his chin. "Oh – my!" Jane's cheeks flooded with color, because she wore not a stitch of clothing, and neither did he! She didn't know where to put her eyes – or her hands!

"Good morning, Mrs Bingley," Charles drawled, guessing quite accurately at her thoughts as Jane screwed her eyes shut. Gently he ran his fingers down the curve of her spine.

"Charles, you must not, you must go," she squeaked. "Helena will be coming in soon, surely..." in the few moments she had her eyes open, Jane had clearly seen that morning light was flooding the room.

"Helena is not foolish enough to enter your rooms until you ring for her now that you are a married lady, Mrs Bingley." She was tense against him, and Charles smoothed his hands up her back again. "Relax, Jane," he whispered in her ear. "Give your husband a kiss."

"Our guests," she said faintly, her resolve to behave in a ladylike manner fading rapidly away under his gentle touch.

"Will not expect to see us at all this day: indeed, if they did they would likely think all was not well with our marriage. Perhaps that I had hurt you."

"Oh, no, you did not at all, Charles!" Jane's eyes flew open. "I – I liked what we did," her voice was very shy, but her aqua eyes met his directly.

"Good, because I have a powerful need to love you again," he told her, grinning, rolling to trap her beneath him. Jane giggled, and then lost all urge to laugh as his mouth came down on hers, hot and hungry and no longer at all frightening.

About half an hour later, Charles finally allowed Jane to ring the bell. Reluctantly he gathered his robe and trousers and returned to his own room, though not before telling Jane that he would order breakfast served in her private parlour and he would come to join her there in a little while. She was stiff and a little sore, he was sure of it from the way she moved though she did not complain, and he was quite sure that she would very much welcome a soothing bath.

"But do not allow Helena to dress you," he kissed her with a hunger that was no less fierce for having been slaked. "Come in your gown and robe, for once we have eaten I will likely need to adjourn to bed again with you."

"Charles," Jane began to argue, turning pink again, and he fisted his hand in the hair at the nape of her neck and kissed her harder.

"And tell her to leave your hair down." He grinned at her outraged expression. "I like to feel it all over me."

"You are shocking," she said with a small smile, "but it is a wife's duty to be

Catherine Bilson

obedient to her husband, and so I will do as you wish."

Charles laughed and headed back to his own room, where his valet already awaited him, alerted by the bell Jane had rung for Helena.

Jane stayed in bed, pulling her gown and robe as straight as she could, unable to suppress her blush as she thought that everyone in the house knew exactly what she and Charles had been up to. And then a moment later Helena came in from the dressing room at the head of a small army of maids. Footmen behind her were already draining last night's bath and pouring fresh hot water for a new one.

In short order Jane was bathed while her bed was changed, the bloodied sheets whisked away, though she knew they would surely be displayed and discussed downstairs. Helena held up a day gown for Jane to consider while she sat in the bath, but Jane, blushing, shook her head.

"No, Helena. Mr Bingley has decreed that we will not go into company today."

"Very good, ma'am," utterly discreet and guessing well at the direction of the

68

master's thoughts, Helena produced a fresh nightgown and wrapper. She did not raise an eyebrow when Jane blushed and asked that her hair be left down after brushing, too. The maid only bowed her head and departed quietly when Jane murmured, "Thank you, Helena, that will be all."

Jane took a deep breath and opened the door to her parlour. Charles looked up at her and smiled. Wearing again his silk trousers and robe, he looked so handsome to her, relaxed on the couch with a cup of tea in hand.

"Tea, my dearest?" he offered.

"I should love some," Jane sat down beside him and accepted the cup he poured for her, adding a dribble of honey just as she liked it. She ran her eyes over the feast arrayed on the small table before them and smiled. "Your cook has done us proud, Charles."

"I think she suspected that perhaps I had worked up an appetite," he said mischievously, and laughed as Jane blushed yet again. "You are so pretty when you blush."

"It is fortunate that is your opinion, because you seem to delight in provoking me!" she retorted. "I did not think that you were such a tease, Mr Bingley!"

"Only with my lovely bride," he said deeply, smiling at her. "Come, my love. Taste this pastry, it is quite delicious."

Charles insisted on feeding Jane delicious morsels of food with his own hands, until she declared herself quite full. And then he scooped her up in his arms, despite her protesting squeal, and carried her to his bed this time.

"Are you sore?" he asked quietly as he laid her down.

Jane hesitated. "Not really?"

He sat back on his heels, looked at her thoughtfully. "Now why do I not quite believe you?"

"I'm not!" Jane insisted. "A little stiff, perhaps, through my... hips." It wasn't an easy word to say aloud, even to one's husband, she discovered. He nodded understandingly, though.

"Unaccustomed exercise," Charles said with a small grin, "can do that to one. Like spending a long day on horseback when one has not ridden for a while."

Jane nodded, grateful for the innocuous comparison. She seemed to have spent almost every minute since her marriage in a permanent state of blush, wondered if she would ever become inured to the events and words which caused her embarrassment. Quite possibly not, she suspected, as her husband gently removed her robe and nightgown to leave her quite bare to his hungry gaze.

"I'll try not to make your hips ache any more," Charles said, a teasing little smile playing about his lips.

"How...?" Jane began, and then realised she really shouldn't have asked as his eyebrows rose.

"I believe I'd rather show than tell," Charles told her with a wicked grin, sliding down the bed, parting her legs and lying down between them. Jane watched wide-eyed as he began to press gentle kisses against her inner thighs, his freshly-shaven jaw smooth against her skin.

"What are you — Charles!" It was a squeak of shock as he pressed an open-mouthed kiss against her most intimate spot. "Oh, my... oh, my goodness!" His blue eyes glinted at her as his tongue flicked, and

71

Jane found that she could not look at him. Grabbing a pillow, she dragged it over her face and shrieked her pleasure into it as Charles continued his work.

When Charles gently pulled the pillow away, a scarlet-faced Jane could not meet his eyes. She turned over, pressed her face into the mattress; squeaked with shock as his hand caressed down the small of her back to lightly pat at her bottom.

"I am sure that is very wicked," she said in a small voice.

"Are you?" He pressed slow kisses along her spine, working his way up from the small of her back, gathering her thick golden hair in his hands to pull it to the side, out of his way. "Why are you so sure?"

She couldn't put words to it. "Something that feels so good must surely be sinful," she said into the bedding at last, feeling goosebumps rise up as he reached the nape of her neck.

"There are quite a number of acts considered sinful when conducted out of wedlock, that are perfectly sanctioned when they occur between husband and wife," Charles said, amused. "In the privacy of our bedroom, my Jane, I want no talk of sin from you." Gently, he put his arm around her slender waist, pulled her back and onto her side to spoon within the curve of his larger body. "Here, there is only love; the intense love I have for you, my wish that you should find only joy in our bed."

"I do," Jane whispered. "I love you too, Charles..."

"Then please, my darling, please trust me. Lovemaking is natural and beautiful; God would not have made your body capable of such pleasures if it were not in His grand design, would He?"

"I suppose not," she conceded, daring a glance back at him as he kissed gently along her shoulder. "Do you — does it feel that way for you too, Charles?"

"Men and women are not the same, so I cannot exactly answer your question, my love. But yes, I think that it does feel very much the same — if it feels like a little glimpse of heaven on earth to you too, that is."

Jane gasped as his hand moved upwards and his fingers began to caress her breasts again, very gently. She could feel the hard bar of his manhood pressing against the small of her back, bit at her lips as that unfamiliar excitement began to well up inside her. "Yes," she said, trying hard to keep her voice steady. "It feels just like heaven, but Charles... I feel so wanton."

He chuckled against her shoulder, leaning further forward to kiss her cheek as his fingers teased and tantalised. "So long as you only feel this way for your husband, my angel, there is no sin."

"Oh, I could not ever consider feeling so with anyone else!" Jane exclaimed, quite shocked.

"Good." His knee edged between hers, nudging her thighs apart as he shifted behind her.

"Even this — this is not sinful?" Jane could not suppress a moan as Charles' hand left her breast, slipping down between her legs, even as he pressed against her from behind.

"Not in the least," Charles reassured breathlessly. "You can relax and enjoy it with a clear conscience."

"Oh, g-good," Jane panted, unable to keep from arching back against him as his manhood pushed slowly back inside her again, "else I should never be able to set foot inside church again!"

Afterwards Jane lay curled up to Charles' side, her slender fingers tracing lightly over the defined muscles of his chest. He smiled blissfully at the ceiling, thinking that he was going to enjoy being married far more than he had ever imagined. One hand traced gently along the sweep of Jane's long golden hair, falling like tumbled silk threads behind her.

"Your hair is so soft," he murmured, feeling almost drunken with pleasure. "I am surely the luckiest man in England right now."

Jane smiled against his skin. "I am surely the luckiest woman," she replied softly.

Turning to his side, meeting her eyes, Charles told her sincerely; "I told you when I came back to you, but I want to say it again. I was a great fool to leave here last November, and I thank God that Elizabeth chanced to come to Derbyshire with your aunt and uncle. The moment I laid eyes on her, I realised that what I had been trying to do was an impossibility; that I could never forget you because you had taken up residence in my heart."

"Oh, Charles." Jane had to blink back threatening tears. "When Lizzy told me that she had seen you, that you had asked so particularly after me — I was afraid to hope."

"I am so sorry for what I did to you, my angel." Gently, he caressed the pure line of her jaw, leaned in to press a kiss to her forehead. "Never again will I allow anything to come between us, I promise you."

Jane smiled as he put his arms around her, tugging her close. "Even clothes, apparently," she said slyly, making Charles burst out laughing.

"Especially not clothes!"

Caroline Makes Mischief

Darcy and Elizabeth, having spent a very blissful night of their own, felt it incumbent on them as guests at Netherfield to rejoin the company at breakfast time. Directly after breakfast, when Darcy excused himself for a short ride – he needed to work off some energy lest he behave disgracefully and carry Elizabeth off to bed again – Caroline Bingley lost no time making several unsubtle digs at Elizabeth about the ill-bred behaviour of her younger sisters the day before.

Kitty *had* carried on like an absolute idiot on meeting Colonel Fitzwilliam, Elizabeth knew, but it was still appallingly rude of Caroline to point it out, particularly since she was now related to Kitty by marriage. Elizabeth considered suggesting that Caroline take Kitty under her wing to teach her to conduct herself in a manner more befitting a lady, but really, Kitty hadn't done anything bad enough to deserve having Caroline inflicted on her. She bit her tongue.

"One could expect no better, I suppose," Caroline sneered, "considering that you yourself, Eliza, displayed a remarkable ignorance in departing before the general company had dispersed yesterday evening!"

Elizabeth blinked in astonishment. "Mr Darcy and I were not the hosts of the gathering, Miss Bingley," she observed coolly.

Miss Darcy happened to be in range to overhear their conversation. "Indeed," she interjected, surprising Elizabeth who hadn't thought the shy girl likely to speak up in her defence, "I observed that it was my brother's choice to depart early, Miss Bingley."

At which remark, Caroline's disappointed hopes peaked in a fit of rage. "Well, we all know that men are unable to control their baser instincts," she said icily, "but I should have thought that Eliza should know it does not do to display too much affection for one's husband in public. Or indeed in private. It is considered most ill-bred."

"Where is your brother this morning, Miss Bingley?" Elizabeth enquired, knowing full well where Charles was. "I should like to see my sister."

Caroline's expression was puce with rage. "Kept from his duties to his guests by the arts and allurements of a wanton woman!" she hissed.

"Are you implying that my sister came to her marriage in a less than chaste condition?" Elizabeth lost her temper. "I warn you, Miss Bingley, if such slander ever reaches Jane's ears, I will... I will..."

"You will what?" Caroline sneered contemptuously.

"*I* will tell my brother, and you may be very sure that you would never be received by any respectable connection of the Darcy family ever again!" It was Georgiana who spoke, utterly horrified by what she was witnessing. "You cannot possibly be implying such a thing about Miss Bennet – Mrs Bingley, now! I have known her only a few days, and she is the sweetest, kindest lady – you should pray to God for forgiveness for saying such dreadful things about her!"

"It's all right, Georgiana," Elizabeth reached for her new sister's hand and squeezed it gently, though her eyes never left Caroline's furiously red face. "It appears that disappointment has caused Miss Bingley to forget her veneer of civility. Obviously, you can take the girl away from the docks, but the docks will remain within her."

Caroline sputtered with rage, but Elizabeth was not finished. "And while I would not expect a young unmarried lady like Miss Darcy to understand the meeting of minds that occur between a husband and wife truly in love with one another, you, Miss Bingley, are somewhat older and have witnessed not only your sister's marriage but surely many of your friends, as well. If you have never seen a married couple who are genuinely fond of each other before, I can only pity your sister and your friends; but you should thank me, and Jane too, for showing you what a marriage can be like when you love and are loved in return. I urge you, Miss Bingley, to settle for nothing less."

There were so many subtle digs in Elizabeth's little speech that Caroline quite simply could not process them all. She stood, open-mouthed, as the new Mrs Darcy tugged lightly on Miss Darcy's hand and led her away.

"Get out!" finding her voice, Caroline shouted the words after the pair. All conversation in the drawing-room was instantly silenced; the Countess of Matlock broke off in the middle of speaking to Mrs Hurst, casting a disbelieving stare at Caroline.

"I beg your pardon, Miss Bingley?" Elizabeth turned around, unable to believe what Caroline had just said.

"I said, *get out*," Caroline hissed at her. "You disgusting, worthless *hussy*!"

"Caroline!" Louisa Hurst shot to her feet, faster than Elizabeth had ever seen the indolent woman move, and hurried to her sister's side. "You are overwrought, my dear, you don't know what you are saying. It's been a very busy few days," she tried to excuse Caroline's behaviour, but the shocked expressions of every lady present told her clearly that she was fighting a losing battle.

Caroline shook free of Louisa's restraining arm, stepped forward to face Elizabeth. "I know exactly what I am saying," she pronounced coldly, "and you will get out of my house now or I will have you thrown from it, Eliza Bennet!"

"She has run mad," Georgiana whispered, beginning to shake with terror as she backed away from the confrontation. Her aunt the countess rose to come to her side, placing herself between Georgiana and Miss Bingley.

"I think you have forgot yourself, Miss Bingley," overcoming her own shock, Elizabeth rose to the challenge. "For not only did I give up the name Bennet to become Mrs Darcy yesterday, but my sister became mistress of Netherfield when she married your brother. I do not believe that you have the *authority* to order me from this house." Her tone was absolutely steady as she faced off bravely against the taller woman.

Caroline let out a screech of pure rage, and her hand swung, far too quickly for Mrs Hurst to stop her. The *crack* of her palm connecting with Elizabeth's cheek echoed like a gunshot in the silent room.

Caroline Bingley was not a small woman, and she had used the full force of her arm. Caught off guard, never thinking for a moment that the other woman would dare to use violence against her, Elizabeth stumbled and fell.

Georgiana screamed. Scarcely able to believe what had just happened, the Countess stepped forward instinctively, intercepted Caroline as the younger woman made to kick at Elizabeth's fallen form.

"Miss Bingley!" she cried. "You forget yourself!"

"Caroline, you must not!" Louisa Hurst tugged at her sister's arm, her face a picture of horror. "Come away, oh please, you must come away..."

"Lizzie!" Georgiana went to her knees, clutching desperately at Elizabeth. "Oh, please, please be all right..."

Elizabeth had fallen awkwardly, putting her arm out to catch herself. She rolled to her back now, cradling her wrist with the other hand, her face pale. "I heard a crack, and it hurts really quite dreadfully," she said through gritted teeth.

"Miss Bingley has gone mad," Georgiana whispered in shock, watching as her aunt and Mrs Hurst hastily pushed a still red-faced but now mercifully silent Caroline from the room.

"I shall not argue, but it is not for us to judge." Painfully, with Georgiana's help, Elizabeth got to her feet, but at once collapsed to sit down on a couch. "Pray ring for a maid, Georgiana. I think we had best send to Meryton for the doctor." She bit down on her lower lip to try and suppress the tears of pain that sprang to her eyes, not wanting to upset an already distressed Georgiana further.

Georgiana surprised Elizabeth, though, firming her spine and crossing the room to pull the bell. "My brother will see that Miss Bingley is punished for this," she promised, suddenly sounding very much like a Darcy of Pemberley to Elizabeth's ears. "Do not fear, Lizzie, I am quite sure that we will never lay eyes on her again."

"I sincerely hope not," Elizabeth said faintly. Her wrist hurt quite abominably; there was a ringing in her ears. Determined not to swoon, she lay back on the couch, resting her head on its cushioned back. It was abominably uncomfortable, and she silently wished down a few more curses on Caroline Bingley's head. Could she not at least have had a weakness for comfortable furniture? Despite her determination, the pain overcame her and she slipped into unconsciousness just as Netherfield's housekeeper and two maids entered the room, alerted that something significant was happening by the spectacle of a screeching Miss Bingley being hustled up the stairs by Mrs Hurst and the Countess.

"Miss Darcy... *Mrs* Darcy!" the housekeeper gasped as Elizabeth slid from the couch to the floor in a dead faint. "Oh, the good Lord preserve us, what has happened here?"

"I pray you remain calm, Mrs Hughes," Georgiana said, her hands shaking but her voice admirably steady. "Mrs Darcy has hurt her arm. Send immediately to Meryton for the doctor, and please send someone to find my brother also."

"Of course, Miss Darcy, at once," soothed by the clear orders, the housekeeper at once sent one of the maids to find footmen to take the messages while she and the other carefully lifted Elizabeth back to the couch, trying to make her comfortable.

"What the devil is going on?" It was Darcy who arrived back first; he had already been on his way back to the house and the footman sent to summon him had found him just dismounting his horse at the stables. He strode into the drawing-room still stripping off his gloves, a forbidding frown on his face. The panicked expression on the footman's face had already alerted him that something was seriously amiss.

"Do not fuss, Will," Elizabeth said weakly from the couch, where she had just regained consciousness under the housekeeper's capable ministrations. "I took a tumble, that is all."

"Is that why I can see the distinct imprint of four fingers on your cheek?" Darcy frowned forbiddingly down at her. "Please tell me it is not what I suspect."

"Miss Bingley *struck* her, Fitzwilliam!" Georgiana exclaimed. The housekeeper sucked in a shocked breath, and Darcy turned his best glare on her.

"The fewer people who hear of *that*, the better."

"Y-yes, Mr Darcy," the housekeeper quavered out. "Nobody will hear it from me, I assure you!"

"Who else was here, Georgiana?" Darcy glanced at his sister, even as he knelt down beside Elizabeth and tenderly stroked her brow.

"Mrs Hurst and Aunt Matlock," Georgiana said, "they both tried to stop Miss Bingley, but... she was beyond reasoning with!"

"Look to Georgiana," Elizabeth whispered to Darcy, "she had a dreadful fright."

Looking from his sister to his new wife, Darcy shook his head. "Stop trying to deflect me, Lizzie. I know you too well; a smack on the cheek would not have you lying down like this with your face white as snow. What has happened, and has the doctor been sent for? I saw young Hodges setting off at a gallop in the direction of Meryton as I was coming in."

"My arm," Elizabeth confessed at last, unable to deny Darcy in such an intent mood. "I fell and there was quite an

Catherine Bilson

unpleasant cracking sound; I fear my wrist might be broken."

Darcy's lips thinned to a tight line; he had to take his hand from Elizabeth's brow for a moment to clench his fists. His voice, when he finally found himself able to speak again, sounded hoarse and strained. "Everything will be fine, beloved, I promise. The doctor will not be too long."

She smiled lovingly at him, instinctively tried to lift her hand to touch his cheek... and fainted dead away again as she unthinkingly moved her injured arm.

The ensuing silence was only broken by the soft thump as Georgiana too slid to the floor in a dead faint.

"Miss Bingley has a *great* deal to answer for," Darcy growled as he hastily rose to scoop up his sister and lay her gently on another couch.

The housekeeper only shook her head incredulously, looking from one lady to the other. "I never heard of such goings-on in all my life," she said frankly.

"I hope nobody else will ever hear of them either," Darcy said darkly, terrifying the woman into silence again. She nodded hastily and fished her smelling-salts out of her apron pocket to try and revive Georgiana.

Bliss, Interrupted

Charles was just considering the beauty of his bride's nude, drowsing form and wondering whether she would feel able to accept his lovemaking yet again when his pleasant musings were interrupted by a quiet, but urgent, tapping at the door that led to his dressing-room.

Frowning, Charles hastily drew some covers over Jane and looked around for his robe, finally finding it discarded on the floor halfway across the room. Shrugging into it, he belted it and headed for the door, opening it a crack to find his valet outside, wringing his hands together anxiously.

"I'm so very sorry to interrupt, sir!"

"What is it, Rogers?" The anxious expression on his normally phlegmatic valet's face had Charles instantly convinced that something was severely amiss.

"It's..." Rogers actually seemed at a loss for words. "Mrs Hurst sent me, sir," he finally settled for saying. "It's Miss Bingley."

"What has Caroline done now?" Charles sighed, saw Rogers' expression change and frowned. "Wait. This is something really bad, isn't it?"

"I don't have all the details, sir. I really think that you should speak to Mrs Hurst."

"All right. Get me some clothes ready, I'll be out in a minute or two."

"Very good, sir!" Rogers looked immensely relieved, which had Bingley shaking his head in bemusement as he closed the door, wondering what on earth Caroline had done to have the household in such an evident uproar.

"What is it, Charles?" Jane asked sleepily from the bed as he turned back towards her.

"Nothing important, my love," but he had never been a good liar, and she immediately sat up in bed, clutching the sheet to her breasts in a display of belated modesty he found utterly arousing, if rather unfortunately timed.

"Charles, that tone in your voice tells me that it *is* something," her aqua eyes were wide, no longer sleepy. "And whatever it is, I am now your wife. Have we not promised to share in all things? If a burden has landed upon your shoulders, please, allow me to share it with you."

"You truly are an angel," he said reverently, and Jane shook her head.

"Never that, my darling, but I *am* your wife."

"So you are, Mrs Bingley, so you are. Well, it seems that Caroline may have done something beyond the pale, though as yet I know not what, and I am summoned to deal with it."

"Whatever could she have done?" Heedless of her nakedness in her urgent desire to be of use, Jane scrambled from the bed and tugged the bell-pull before looking around for her gown and robe. Charles had to turn away before he forgot himself entirely.

"I do not know, but I am sure that Louisa would not have sent Rogers to disturb me unless it were really quite serious. I hesitate to speculate." Unfortunately, he had a fairly good notion of what exactly might have led Caroline to extreme action, and her name was now Mrs Elizabeth Darcy.

"Do not go without me, I pray you," Jane begged, shrugging into her robe and belting it hastily. "I will have Helena dress me as quickly as she may!"

He was not about to refuse her anything, especially not when she looked so utterly fetching with her long golden hair tumbling around her shoulders like that. "I will wait for you to be ready, I promise."

Charles was nonetheless impressed when Jane re-entered the bedroom a scant ten minutes later, wearing a pretty round gown and with her hair neatly coiled and pinned. Turning from the window where he had just been watching the doctor's gig driving swiftly up to Netherfield's front entrance, he smiled at her and offered his arm.

"How pretty you look, Mrs Bingley!"

Jane smiled, but did not blush at the compliment as she might have just a day or so earlier. It took a good deal more to shock her now that she was a wife, she reflected, as she took Charles' arm and they exited their suite together.

"I just saw Doctor Thomas arrive," Charles murmured to Jane as they came to the head of the stairs and heard voices below. "I think perhaps we should go below and see why he is here, before we go to see Louisa and Caroline."

"Certainly! If someone is taken ill, our first priority must be their comfort," Jane agreed immediately.

They proceeded below in perfect accord, both concerned with the comfort of their friends and guests more than that of their own, though it would certainly not be true to say that neither of them resented the intrusion into their idyllic day. Indeed, both of them quietly but heartily wished Caroline Bingley anywhere but at Netherfield, disrupting the very first day of their married life together.

The doctor was just being admitted to the parlour as they arrived at the foot of the stairs; they followed him in to see Elizabeth and Georgiana both prostrate and unconscious.

"What in God's name," Charles started, but was cut off by Jane's shriek of horror as she let go his arm and darted to her sister's side.

"Lizzy, darling Lizzy, whatever has happened? And poor Georgiana, oh my..."

"Miss Bennet — Mrs Bingley, calm yourself, I beg you," the doctor put a paternal hand on her arm, guiding her gently aside. "Please, allow me to examine my patients." He looked from Georgiana to Elizabeth, and then at Darcy. "Uh, Mr Darcy, would you care to enlighten me on what exactly has transpired?"

"Georgiana has fainted," Darcy filled him in succinctly, "as has Elizabeth, but I believe that Elizabeth's arm may be broken. She suffered a fall and hurt her arm."

The doctor looked at the reddened finger-marks on Elizabeth's cheek and frowned severely at Darcy. "Suffered a fall," he said disbelievingly.

"I was not present, sir," Darcy's expression and tone grew ever more forbidding. "I was summoned to my wife's side only to find Mrs Darcy and my sister both in the most severe distress."

Georgiana's eyelashes fluttered open just then at the housekeeper's continued efforts, and Jane decided that she would be most of use attending to the younger girl while the doctor concentrated his efforts on Elizabeth.

Charles drew Darcy aside, though the other man clearly had no intention of straying more than a step or two from Elizabeth's side.

"What in God's name is going on here, Darcy?" Charles hissed at his friend. "Rogers summoned me with some urgent message that Caroline had made mischief..." he put it together then, adding the finger-marks on Elizabeth's cheek to the message, and fairly gasped. "*No.* No, even Caroline would not..."

"I was not here, Bingley, but Georgiana saw it all. Caroline struck Elizabeth, and she fell."

"No," Charles said again, but weakly, in the face of Darcy's steady look. "Oh, dear God."

"You've turned positively green, don't you dare faint on me too," Darcy said in horror, pressing Bingley to a seat.

"I'm not going to faint, but I may lose my breakfast! I am so sorry, Darcy, I cannot even *begin* to imagine what Caroline was thinking!"

"It is not your fault," Darcy said quietly. "We both knew how much she despised Elizabeth, and you *did* speak to her sternly,

97

seek to rein her in. If I'd suspected even for a moment that she might be so reckless as to try to harm my wife, I should never have left Lizzy alone."

Charles pressed his fingers to his brow, thinking frantically. "I must speak to Louisa." Looking at Jane, kneeling beside Georgiana and speaking to her softly, he said "Please be assured, Darcy, that Jane and I will put Elizabeth's comfort as our highest priority. I am deeply ashamed that such an incident could have occurred under my roof."

Darcy's stern expression softened, and he reached to put his hand on Bingley's shoulder. "I do not doubt it, Bingley. Even if you were foolish enough to think otherwise, Mrs Bingley would soon set you straight."

"She most certainly would." Resolute, Charles rose to his feet. "I will get to the bottom of this, Darcy, and whatever happens you have my word that Caroline will be gone from this house by nightfall."

Darcy offered his hand for a silent shake before returning to Elizabeth's side. Jane, seeing that they had finished their conversation, rose to her feet with a gently reassuring pat to Georgiana's hand.

"Charles?" she enquired, the single word conveying volumes.

"I must go and confer with Louisa." He shook his head at her look of concern. "I fear I still do not have the complete story, my love, but what little I do know indicates that Caroline has brought tremendous shame on herself, and by extension her family."

Jane pressed her lips together before nodding and squaring her shoulders. "Then we must do whatever is within our power to make amends for her actions," she said steadily.

"My angel." Here in company with Georgiana's innocent eyes upon them, he contented himself with a light press of his fingers against hers. "Please, stay here and see that Miss Darcy and Elizabeth are afforded every care. The staff are entirely at your disposal."

"Of course." She gave him a calm, regal nod.

"I will deal with Caroline."

Jane's next words surprised him. "I know that she is your sister, Charles, but do not allow yourself to be swayed. Her selfish actions have almost cost us too much already."

Her eyes and expression were quite calm, but that serene attitude was only a cover for a will of iron, Charles was beginning to realise. He lifted her hand to his lips and placed a kiss on her fingertips.

"Your wish is my command, my angel."

He was rewarded with Jane's radiant smile before she turned away to attend to Georgiana again. Charles held his head high as he strode from the room, determined to live up to Jane's faith in him.

Confrontation

Perhaps Charles' resolve would have weakened on his way up the stairs had it not been for the lingering memory of Jane's last smile at him. Instead, he marched straight up to the door of Caroline's suite and rapped on it sharply.

"Who is it?" Louisa's voice called.

"Charles," he replied loudly. "Open the door, Louisa." He was proud of himself for keeping his tone stern; he must have sounded extremely displeased because Louisa, far from keeping him waiting as was usually her wont, opened the door almost instantly.

"Where is she?" Charles asked.

"In her bedroom." There were tears streaming down Louisa's cheeks. "Oh *Charles*," she sobbed brokenly, "I think she has run mad!"

Awkwardly, Charles opened his arms and Louisa positively threw herself into them, clinging to his coat and sobbing against his chest.

"I'm sorry, I'm sorry," she sniffled out as he patted her back, trying to comfort her. "Please don't think that I feel as she does, I do not. Jane is an angel, really she is, and I am so happy for you..."

"We both know that Jane isn't the root of the problem," Charles said gently. "Don't we?"

Louisa nodded, looking up at him from teary eyes. "She hates Elizabeth so much, Charles, it is truly frightening... I think she might do something awful. *More* awful," she corrected herself. "Whatever shall we do? If Mr Darcy's aunt the Countess ever chooses to speak of what Caroline did, our family would never be able to show our faces in society again!"

"The Countess won't speak of it as long as Caroline is suitably dealt with." Charles hoped that was true; Darcy had given his word and he would surely convince his aunt to keep her silence as long as Charles ensured that Caroline had no further opportunity to harm Elizabeth.

"What does that mean? I'll support you, Charles, whatever you decide, but what can we possibly do?"

He had been wondering that, turning over possible options in his head all the way up the stairs. "I believe that we must send her to Sir John and Lady Forrest. I will write to Sir John apprising him of the true facts of the matter, so that they will know not to believe any wild nonsense Caroline may spout."

Louisa drew in a deep breath and squared her shoulders. "I think Gerald and I should escort her. I feel that I must share in the blame for this, Charles; I encouraged her to pursue Mr Darcy, after all."

"You did not encourage her once his engagement was announced, though," Charles said dryly. "I distinctly recall overhearing you telling her to let it go and set her sights on a new target."

"Caroline never was inclined to listen to good advice," Louisa said, accepting his handkerchief to wipe her eyes. "Still, I should like to do this. I can speak to Sir John and Lady Forrest myself. Gerald would like to see Sir John again, I am sure... and this will give you time to spend alone with your new bride."

Charles was surprised at the twinkle that appeared in Louisa's eye with that last remark. Smiling fondly down at her, he bent to kiss her cheek. "You are considerate, dear sister."

"Well, I have not always been so, but I shall seek to take my example from Mrs Bingley from now on." Louisa took a deep breath and wiped at her eyes once more. "I shall direct the maids to begin packing."

He kissed her cheek again and allowed her to escape. Her presence at the coming confrontation could only be undesirable; Caroline would resent Louisa witnessing the dressing-down she was about to receive.

She was standing by the window, quite alone, for which he was grateful. He hadn't thought to ask if the Countess remained with her, hoped devoutly that Darcy's aunt could be persuaded to keep her silence on the matter.

"Well, this is a fine mess you've made of things," he said eventually when Caroline did not deign to acknowledge his entry into the room.

"I could say the same of you," she responded loftily.

"Caroline, I don't think you realise the magnitude of your offence! You struck a member of the peerage's family; Elizabeth has a *broken arm*. If Darcy chose to, he could have you taken up by the magistrate for assault."

Caroline glanced at him; Charles barely recognised her. Her face was as still and cold as marble, her eyes fathomless dark pools. "She is faking it, the lying slut."

"She is *not* faking it!" It was very rare for Charles Bingley to lose his temper, but he did so now, striding forward, grasping Caroline's shoulders in his hand and giving her a firm shake. "Your jealousy has blinded you to reason, Caroline, and you are on the edge of ruining yourself in the eyes of society forever, do you not see that?"

She stared at him, her brow creasing in puzzlement. "Why aren't you taking my side over hers?"

"Because your actions are unconscionable!" He shouted it, saw her eyes widen as she realised that for once, there was no way that she could convince him to take her side. "Striking even a servant is a disgraceful act; to strike a lady who is now your superior in consequence is quite beyond the pale! If the countess chooses to speak of it in society you will be ruined, Caroline. *Ruined*. And *she* has no reason in the slightest to care about safeguarding your good name."

Finally, the magnitude of her offence seemed to dawn on Caroline, because she paled and bit her lip. "Will you speak to her?"

"I will, but frankly I am more concerned about the damage Louisa, Jane and I could suffer because of your thoughtless actions, than about you!"

She looked more annoyed by that than understanding, and Charles sighed and let go of her shoulders. There was no reasoning with Caroline, he saw; the time had passed for that.

"Darcy will not countenance the sight of you," he said flatly, forging on despite her gasp of outrage. "He was prepared to tolerate you while you maintained your veneer of civility, for my sake, but your attack on Elizabeth has ended that. Frankly, I do not trust not you to behave in some vicious manner towards Jane, too."

"I would..."

"You will be silent." He no longer cared to hear her excuses. Ignoring her gaping mouth as he spoke over her, he said "Louisa has been kind enough to offer to escort you to visit Sir John and Lady Forrest in Scarborough, and there you will remain, Caroline. I will pay your allowance direct to Sir John from this day forward, as credit towards your room and board. Henceforth, you are not welcome in any house in which Mrs Bingley and I reside, and you would do very well to ensure that you do not ever again come to Mr Darcy's notice."

"You cannot mean it." Her voice shook.

"Every word." He met her eyes unflinchingly. "You will reside with the Forrests until I give you leave, Caroline. I advise you to be extremely circumspect in Scarborough. Should word of your exploits reach so far north, you would be ostracised from even that limited social circle." Turning away, he headed for the door. "Louisa has already directed the maids to begin your packing. I gave Darcy my word that you would be leaving before nightfall, and I do not intend to renege on that promise."

Tears started in her eyes as she gazed at his implacable expression and she reached out a hand imploringly, but Charles shook his head.

"This is the result of your own actions, Caroline. I can only hope that you can find it in you to be happy in the bed you have made for yourself."

She stood silent as he left the room, but as Charles closed the door behind him, he heard a scream of rage and the crash of something heavy hitting the door. Sighing deeply, he headed for his study. He had a letter to write.

Mutual Support

Charles cursed and dropped his pen into the inkwell, uncaring of the ink that splashed onto his desk. Running his hands into his hair, he tugged hard, silently berating himself. He was a poor correspondent at the best of times, and this was an exceedingly difficult letter to write. How did one impose upon a man related to one only by marriage to take your most impossible relative off your hands before she ruined your family name permanently?

"Charles," a soft hand touched his wrist, and he startled. He hadn't heard Jane enter; looked up to see her standing beside him now, concern etched on her lovely face as she looked at the blotched and crumpled papers strewn on his desk.

Without even pausing to consider how she might react, he put his arms around her and pulled her into his lap, pressing his face into her soft, sweet-scented golden hair. Jane stiffened only briefly before relaxing against him, though, slipping her arms around his neck.

"What is it?" she asked quietly. "Let me help you, please, my love."

"I am a poor letter-writer anyway, as Darcy will be at pains to tell you," Charles sighed, "and this is an exceptionally difficult subject."

"So I see." Jane looked again at the mess on his desk. "Perhaps... you could dictate to me, and I could write the letter for you? Then all you have to do is sign it."

Startled, he pulled back to look at her. "You are not my secretary, Jane!"

She smiled and took a handkerchief from her pocket, leaning in to dab at his cheek. Despairingly, he realised that he must have ink there too. "No, I am not. I do not think this is business a secretary could be trusted with, even if you had one, but I assure you that I have many times written letters for my father and mother, as well as maintaining correspondences of my own with distant friends and relatives. I have a fair hand."

"I have no doubt that it is as fair as everything else about you," he acquiesced.

"Thank you, my love, I will accept your offer. Otherwise, it is highly unlikely that this letter would be ready to go when the Hursts must depart."

Jane smiled and rose to her feet. "Let us clear away this mess and begin anew, then," she suggested, gathering the crumpled and blotted papers, throwing them into the fireplace. "Dear me, whatever have you done to this pen?"

He smiled sheepishly at her and offered his handkerchief to clean up the splattered ink, gladly giving up his seat to pace the room and try to think of the words he would need to use.

Jane settled herself with a fresh sheet of paper and pen, first testing it on a scrap she had saved to see how well it worked. "So, who is the letter to?" she enquired.

"Oh... Sir John Forrest. I suppose you should begin with *My dear Sir John.*"

For a minute the only sounds in the room were the crackle of the flames and the scratch of Jane's pen. Charles admired the way she looked, golden head bent over the paper.

"What next?" Jane asked.

"Oh!" He startled guiltily, realising that he had been quite lost in his perusal of his wife's beauty.

"Perhaps wishes for his good health and our thanks for the gift he and Lady Forrest sent for our wedding?" Jane suggested.

"The exceedingly ugly porcelain clock?"

Jane's lips twitched. "I was not going to describe it in precisely those terms."

"I would, but I have no doubt that you will surpass me in tactful description as you do in everything else." Charles found himself smiling at her. She chuckled gently at him, shaking his head before bending back to the letter.

"Let me just take care of that, then, while you think about the information you need to convey."

By the time she looked up again, he had his thoughts in some sort of order, and dictated a polite letter requesting that Sir John accept Caroline into his household for the immediate future. He did not wish to commit exact details of Caroline's actions to paper, but suggested that she had committed a serious infraction and that Sir John should ask Louisa for the details.

"I shall direct my banker to forward to you the full amount of Caroline's allowance," Charles finally warmed to his subject, the words flowing more easily now that he did not have to focus on writing them down. "I leave its distribution to your discretion, but please ensure that she is not able to accumulate sufficient funds to depart your household."

Jane paused in her industrious scratching. "Do you really think Caroline would run away?" she asked.

"I do not know," Charles said bleakly. "When we spoke above stairs, I hardly recognised her, Jane; I fear that her jealousy and disappointment has damaged her sanity. I can only hope that some time away from society, time to rest and reflect upon her actions, may wreak a change in her."

"I hope so too," Jane said quietly, returning to her writing. Charles reflected that it was the first time he had heard Jane actually voice a criticism of Caroline, despite Caroline's mean actions towards her.

"How is Elizabeth?" Suddenly, he realised that he had not thought to ask, cursed himself guiltily. "And Miss Darcy?"

"Miss Darcy is merely overwrought, her aunt the Countess has her in hand. Elizabeth's wrist is broken. Doctor Thomas placed splints upon it and Mr Darcy carried her to their suite."

Charles kneaded at his forehead, retuning to Jane's side. Her voice had remained admirably calm and steady as she recited the information, but he thought he knew her well enough by now to suspect that Jane appeared the most calm when she was feeling the strongest emotions.

"Darcy will see to her comfort, my love. She will have the best of care, and Caroline will never be in a position to hurt her again." Gently, he placed his hand on her shoulder.

Setting her pen down, Jane reached up to put her hand on his, turning her eyes up to him beseechingly. "Do you promise me that, Charles? Lizzy is the dearest person in the world to me, after you of course, but Caroline is *your* sister..."

"She is also in the wrong, and she has made it very evident that I must take steps to protect others from future consequences of her venom," Charles assured her. "I solemnly promise, dearest, that I will do whatever I must to ensure she can never again harm Elizabeth, nor any other person dear to us."

Jane turned her head and kissed his fingers, whispering a soft "Thank you," before reaching to pick up the pen again.

They completed the letter together, Jane making suggestions when Charles struggled to find the words to express himself. She handed him the pen to make his signature at the bottom of the paper, laughing when he said he feared he would blot her beautiful handiwork.

"It is only a letter, Charles, and one that by necessity is written in haste."

"It looks like a work of art," Charles admired her delicate handwriting. "I had never seen your writing before today."

"Had you not? No, I suppose I have had neither cause nor opportunity to write to you." Carefully sanding the note and folding it for Charles to affix his seal, Jane smiled.

"I shall write you a love letter — and do not fear, I shall not expect a written response!"

"That is good, because I fear you should be waiting for a long time." He smiled guiltily, tucking the finished letter into his pocket. "You shall have to make do with my regular assurance that you have my ardent and undying adoration."

"Well, when you put it like that, I believe that I shall be quite satisfied," Jane blushed prettily, and Charles could not help pulling her into his arms for a kiss.

The Countess

A knock on the study door made them spring apart, Jane flushing guiltily. Charles chuckled at her as she patted her hair and fanned her cheeks, trying in vain to look composed.

"A husband may kiss his wife in private, you know," he told her, crossing to the door. She only cast him a reproachful look, making him smile again as he opened the door to find Mr Hurst there.

"A word, Charles?" Gerald said gruffly, entering the room at his gesture. "Oh," he stopped on seeing Jane. "Beg your pardon, Mrs Bingley, I did not know you were in here."

"That's quite all right, Mr Hurst, and please, won't you call me Jane? We are family now, after all."

Hurst's scowling expression lightened as she moved to stand at Charles' side. "That we are, and I'm glad that Charles came to his senses and returned here for you, Jane. I told him when we quit

Netherfield last year that he shouldn't go without securing your hand."

"You did?" Startled, Jane looked to Charles. She had never realised that she'd had an ally in Mr Hurst.

"Of course I did," Hurst affirmed, and Charles nodded, reaching to clap the other man on the shoulder.

"You did indeed, and I only wish I had listened to you, Gerald. I could have been united in wedded bliss with my angel much sooner."

A knowing smile split Hurst's red face before he sobered. "Yes, well, your wedded bliss is what Louisa and I are called upon to safeguard now, is it not? I must say that I never thought Caroline capable of such venom, but what's done is done. Louisa has all in hand with the packing and your coachman tells me that he will be ready to leave in an hour. We'll not make Peterborough tonight, so by your leave I'll send a rider on to St. Neots to secure rooms for us there."

"Of course," Charles said, thinking guiltily that he should have thought of that himself. "I'll see to it now." Remembering the letter, he drew it from his pocket. "Can I charge you with delivering this to Sir John?"

"Of course." Hurst accepted the letter. "I take it there are some details you haven't committed to paper?"

"Indeed," Charles nodded confirmation. "I must rely upon you and Louisa to give Sir John and Lady Forrest the true facts of the story, and ensure that Caroline is not allowed to twist matters to cast herself in a favourable light."

"Can't see how striking Mrs Darcy could ever be cast in a favourable light, no matter how many fancy words it's hedged around with," Hurst said bluntly.

"And yet, I am confident that if anyone could manage it, Caroline is that person." Charles shook his head. "I will not risk it, Gerald."

"You can count on me, Charles." Hurst hesitated, and then said in a quiet, almost humble tone, "After we have seen Caroline settled with the Forrests, may we return here, Charles?"

"Of course you must!" Jane spoked before a startled Charles could find the words. "I shall depend upon Louisa's help to help me learn the reins here at Netherfield, and I know how much Charles values your company, Gerald."

A smile cracked Hurst's red face, and he picked up Jane's hand and kissed it, much to her surprise. "Spoken like a true lady, Mrs Bingley." He gave her a deep bow before releasing her hand, and saying "By your leave." He departed their presence with a brisker gait and more upright stance than Charles had ever seen from his brother-in-law.

"I think," Charles said thoughtfully, "that I am not the only member of this family who is changed for the better by your mere presence, beloved."

Jane shook her head, placing her hand on his arm. "You are forgetting Caroline, dearest. If Gerald is changing for the better, then Caroline has changed for the worse."

"Perhaps." Leaning in to kiss her cheek, he said "I must go and give orders at the stables, send a rider to reserve rooms... and another ahead to Scarborough, to let Sir John and Lady Forrest know that they will have unexpected guests."

"I will go to see if there is anything that I can do for Miss Darcy or Elizabeth's comfort," Jane said.

"Once you are done with that, my angel, can I invite you to meet me in our suite for luncheon?" Bingley asked hopefully. "We were interrupted earlier, after all."

Jane giggled, blushing pink as his arm tightened around her and he pulled her close. "We shall see. I must see to our guests first, after all."

"Your father is right; we are both far too considerate of the feelings of others for our own good," Charles said regretfully.

"For the first time in my life, I am rather regretting my habit of being nice to everyone," Jane giggled again as Charles rained kisses on her brow and cheeks. "I shall endeavour to ensure everyone's comfort as quickly as I may, beloved."

He rewarded her promise with a thorough kissing, delaying both of their departure for several more minutes, and causing Jane to have to sit down for another minute or two to regain her breath once Charles had departed.

After a little while, she felt herself composed to face company, and left the sanctuary of the study. It was perhaps fortunate that she passed a large mirror in the hall before meeting anyone, though, because her hair was sadly mussed. She paused to straighten it quickly before hurrying abovestairs, proceeding first to Miss Darcy's rooms.

Tapping gently at the door, she was bid to enter, and found Miss Darcy sitting with her aunt the Countess.

"I do beg your pardon, my lady," Jane sank into a low curtsy. "I just wished to see how Miss Darcy was feeling."

"Foolish, Mrs Bingley," Georgiana said with a shy smile, "for fainting when 'twas Mrs Darcy who was the one actually injured."

"It was a deeply shocking event, my dear," Lady Matlock patted her hand. "At your age, I am quite sure that I too would have swooned to the floor!"

Jane, who had witnessed arguments between her sisters take a turn for the physical many a time — Lydia in particular was prone to dealing out slaps when thwarted — nodded sympathetically but said nothing.

"Doctor Thomas seems like a very sensible sort, he knew exactly what to do for Mrs Darcy's arm. I remember my son Richard breaking his arm falling off his horse when he was about your age, Georgiana, and it was splinted and wrapped in just the same way."

"It was?"

"Indeed, and it healed perfectly well."

"Nobody could doubt that, having met Colonel Fitzwilliam!" Georgiana was brought to a proper smile by the Countess' little story.

"Quite, so I do not doubt that in a few weeks Mrs Darcy will be perfectly fine again," Lady Matlock gave a decisive nod, as though the matter was quite settled. Perhaps if you were a Countess, matters did just have a tendency to fall out exactly the way you wished, Jane mused.

"I also take it that there is no possibility of such an incident ever being repeated?" Lady Matlock fixed her with a gimlet eye.

"Indeed not, my lady," Jane hurried to assure her. "Mr and Mrs Hurst are even now preparing to escort Miss Bingley to the home of Sir John and Lady Forrest in Scarborough; Lady Forrest is my husband's former stepmother. Miss Bingley will remain with the Forrests for the foreseeable future."

"I am glad to hear that suitable steps are being taken," was all Lady Matlock said, but she also gave Jane a regal nod and the hint of an approving smile, which in the circumstances Jane felt was all that she might expect. She gave the two ladies another deep curtsy.

"Mr Bingley and I wish to offer our deepest regrets that this terrible incident happened beneath our roof," she said with great sincerity.

"No blame attaches to you, Mrs Bingley, surely," Georgiana exclaimed, "you could not possibly have known!"

"Indeed," Lady Matlock said, "you are not the only one in this room blessed with an impossible sister-by-marriage." She gave Jane a surprisingly sisterly smile, and a wink. "I find myself grateful for the long miles that separate Matlock from Rosings Park."

It suddenly dawned on Jane that Lady Matlock could only be speaking of Lady Catherine de Bourgh. She had to hide a little gasp of shock behind her fingers. Georgiana, too, was gaping at her aunt. Lady Matlock smiled and reached to pat Georgiana's hand.

"One finds with such difficult relatives that the best solution is to keep them at as great a distance as possible. Do not fear, Georgiana, your uncle and I are well aware of your Aunt de Bourgh's nonsensical threats to remove you from your brother's guardianship and we should never have allowed it to come to pass. Your uncle is the head of our family, just as Mr Bingley is the head of his, and we must trust them to manage the more difficult members of it appropriately." She looked at Jane with that sisterly little smile again. "Guided by their wives, of course."

"Of course," Jane echoed, thinking that she was going to like Lady Matlock very much. The Countess had seemed formidable at first, but her solidarity in the face of adversity was like a healing balm to Jane's wounded heart.

"You too are family now, Mrs Bingley," Lady Matlock said in a further surprising twist, "since your sister is married to my nephew. I hope you will remember that, should you ever need to call upon my aid."

There wasn't a lot Jane could say to that, other than, "Your ladyship is too generous," and drop an even deeper curtsy. Lady Matlock gave her a gently dismissive nod and another smile, and Jane departed with a much lighter heart than she had entered with.

Lizzie

Doctor Thomas was just exiting the Darcy suite when Jane got to the door.

"Miss Bennet... I do beg your pardon, Mrs Bingley," he bowed slightly to her.

"How does my sister, Doctor?" Jane had little patience for niceties at that moment. "Please, tell me that she will be well, and soon, I beg of you!"

He looked at her kindly over his half-moon glasses, smiled a little. "Not so soon as we both would wish, but yes, my dear. Elizabeth will soon be well. In my experience, broken bones of the type Mrs Darcy has sustained take perhaps four weeks to begin to heal, and closer to two months for the patient to be completely recovered."

"Two months!" Jane made a horrified face. "Oh, dear!"

"Please allow me to assure you, just as I have just told Mr Darcy, that it need not prevent Mrs Darcy from continuing with her regular activities, in the main. Mrs

Darcy is fortunate to have a maid to help her bathe and dress, by far the most difficult activities with such an injury. She may still walk, and read, and even write letters, since it is her left hand that is injured and not her right. No needlework for the time being though, I am afraid."

"Lizzy never cared so much for needlework anyway," Jane said with a small smile, reassured just as the doctor had intended. "But is she in much pain, Doctor? Is there anything I can do for her?"

"I have given her a little syrup of poppy in a glass of wine, and I shall return tomorrow to see how she does. Until then, I believe that she is in the best of hands with her husband, my dear." The doctor patted her hand soothingly before departing.

Jane hesitated outside the door, wondering if she should just leave Elizabeth and Darcy alone; but her love for her sister compelled her to be sure that Elizabeth was made as comfortable as she could possibly be. A little timidly, she tapped at the door.

The door was opened by Barnes, Mr Darcy's austere and rather intimidating valet. Jane had met the man only a few times, and he was in Mr Darcy's employ rather than that of Netherfield, so she had no authority over him whatsoever. Meekly, she asked;

"Please might I see Mrs Darcy, Barnes?"

The valet looked down his long nose at her before saying "I shall see if Mr Darcy will permit a brief visit, Mrs Bingley."

Jane supposed that she should be grateful he didn't quite shut the door in her face, but left it ajar while he went to speak with Darcy. It was Darcy himself who returned, opening the door and giving her a tight little smile.

"Jane," he said, in not unkind tones, and the tears she'd been holding in for some time now finally began to slip down Jane's cheeks.

"I'm so sorry," she sobbed, and Darcy sighed wearily, put his arm around her shoulders and drew her into the room.

"Sit down, Jane." He pressed her into a chair, put his handkerchief into her hand. "Lizzy is sleeping, the doctor assures me that she will be fine."

"But it's the day after your wedding!" Jane cried, "you should be..." she blushed, thinking of what she and Charles had planned to do all day. "Well, you should be together, celebrating, not..."

"I know, but we cannot always have what we want." Darcy seated himself opposite her, looked at her earnestly. "Sometimes things happen that are beyond our control, and this is one of those things. Neither you nor Charles are to blame for Miss Bingley's actions; indeed, I know that Charles laid down certain stringent conditions to her before your wedding, in the hopes of reining in her behaviour."

"He did?" Jane's eyes opened wide.

"He did, but I admit that I do not know the precise details." Darcy smiled a little more genuinely at her. "I know only that he sought to protect both you and Elizabeth from her spite, and that clearly her own rage and vitriol won out over her better self."

"I am not sure that Caroline *has* a better self," Jane said, and then clapped a hand over her mouth, looking horrified that she had even thought such a thing.

Darcy actually laughed, his eyes twinkling with amusement. "Ah, Jane. That could have been said by my Lizzy herself."

"It was a rather Lizzy thing to say, wasn't it?" Jane gave him a slightly watery smile, wiped at her eyes once more. "Perhaps after all these years she is rubbing off on me a little."

"In my eyes, there can be no such thing as too much Elizabeth." Darcy reached out, gave her hand a gently reassuring touch. "Jane, please do not worry about Lizzy. Her care is my responsibility and I will see to it with every resource at my disposal."

She took a deep breath. "Every resource at Netherfield is at your disposal, then, and that includes myself, should Lizzy require nursing. I could not possibly do less for her than she once did for me."

Darcy actually choked up for a moment. "Her sisterly affection for you was what first endeared her to me," he said a little huskily. "When I saw how devoted she was to your care during your illness."

They smiled mistily at each other before Jane wiped at her eyes again and tucked Darcy's handkerchief into her sleeve, promising to launder and return it. He waved away her promise with a warm smile.

"We are brother and sister now; I cannot tell you how many pocket-handkerchiefs I have lost to Georgiana's clutches. Barnes makes sure I am never without."

Jane smiled. "Should you require anything, anything at all, please have Barnes or Lizzy's maid request it of the housekeeper. I shall inform her that Lizzy's needs are the first priority of this household until she is recovered fully."

She was quite surprised when Darcy claimed her hand and kissed it.

"It is the day after your wedding too, Jane," he told her, "and you should be spending it with your husband. Go and find Charles; he will need your loving comfort more than any of us just now. Whatever else Miss Bingley might be, she is still his sister."

Accepting finally Darcy's assurances that Elizabeth was already receiving the best of care, Jane took her leave. She was lucky enough to find the housekeeper just at the top of the stairs, supervising

Caroline's trunks being carried down to be loaded into the carriage. Drawing her aside briefly, Jane gave instructions that Mr Darcy's requests were to be given the highest possible priority and that anything he might request be provided to him immediately.

"Of course, Mrs Bingley," Mrs Hughes bobbed a respectful curtsy. "Would you like me to station a maid to sit outside their suite, so that she will be on hand in case anything should be required?"

"Excellent suggestion, Mrs Hughes, I shall leave it in your capable hands."

The housekeeper beamed at her, obviously delighted by the small gesture of trust. Jane had seen enough of Caroline's style of managing Netherfield's staff to know that a gentler hand would come as a welcome relief.

"Is she still the same, Gladys?" Mrs Hughes checked with a passing maid; when she answered in the affirmative, the housekeeper turned back to Jane. "Mr and Mrs Hurst went down just a few minutes ago, ma'am, but Miss Bingley has declined to leave her rooms."

Jane stared back at her for a moment before her jaw firmed. "Where is my husband?" she asked.

"Your suite, I believe, ma'am."

"Good; he does not need to be a witness to this. Pray, would you kindly have someone collect our two largest footmen?"

Mrs Hughes' eyes widened, and then she began to smile. "Gladly, ma'am!" She hurried off to do Jane's bidding herself.

Within moments, she returned with two strapping young men trailing at her heels. "Andrew and Alfred, Mrs Bingley," she said. They both bowed deeply. Jane suspected they were brothers; they had a very similar look about them.

"Please follow me," she said, "and do anything I instruct you to. Remember that I am mistress of Netherfield now, and that Miss Bingley is leaving; she will *not* be returning. No matter what she may say, she has no power to punish you."

"Aye, ma'am," Andrew agreed, and Alfred nodded. The pair of them looked almost as pleased as Mrs Hughes; the housekeeper followed along as well as Jane entered Caroline's suite without bothering to knock at the door.

Catherine Bilson

Departure

Caroline's bedchamber was a scene of chaos, Caroline screaming like a fishwife at two maids who were trying to pack her things, grabbing dresses out of trunks and flinging them about the room so that they had to pick them up all over again. Shocked, Jane stopped dead for a moment, just surveying the scene, before gathering herself.

Clapping her hands together sharply, Jane shouted "Stop this nonsense at once!"

Caroline fell silent mid-screech, turning to face Jane with her mouth still hanging open like a carp.

"You need not pick up those gowns, Agnes," Jane said steadily as one of the maids took advantage of the sudden ringing silence to dart forward and grab up a couple of dresses. "If Miss Bingley does not want to take them with her, she need not."

Caroline smirked victoriously. "There, I told you that I would not be leaving!"

"Oh no," Jane said. "You *are* leaving. But you are quite correct that you will not need such ornate gowns as these; I understand that Sir John and Lady Forrest live quite retired. I am sure that Mrs Hurst can make use of some of these in your absence... indeed, this yellow silk will suit Kitty quite well, I shall have it made over for her."

Quite frozen with rage for a moment as Jane took the gown from Agnes and held it up to admire, Caroline could not believe what she was hearing, nor the calm, matter-of-fact tone Jane used to deliver the words.

"How dare you!" she shouted finally. "You jumped-up little nobody, your horrid sister certainly will not have any of my things!"

Jane draped the gown over her arm and fixed Caroline with a level stare. "You forget yourself, Caroline. Your actions today have shown Charles and I that you are not fit to be in charge of any decisions; you have no idea how to behave in a civil manner, in society or out of it. Frankly, I want no part of you. Get out of my house."

Caroline was so shocked she could not move. Jane took a step forward, standing almost nose to nose with her, no fear whatsoever in her expression. Unconsciously, Caroline took a step back; where had quiet, pliable Miss Bennet gone? This woman was confident, secure in her position; Caroline could not intimidate her.

"I said, *get out of my house*," Jane repeated, enunciating her words very clearly. "You can leave on your own two feet and maintain some measure of your dignity, or I will have Alfred and Andrew carry you out bodily. The choice is yours."

Caroline's mouth worked, but she could make no words emerge. Dropping her gaze from those implacably calm aqua eyes, she looked at her maid. "Finish packing those things, Betty..."

"No," Jane interrupted. "You have quite enough, I believe. You will leave now."

"But..." Barely a third of her belongings had been packed and taken downstairs, since Caroline had been doing her level best to impede the process.

"Now." Jane pointed to the door, her expression calm but implacable. "If you are not walking down those stairs by the time I

139

reach the count of ten, you will be going down them over Alfred's shoulder. One. Two. Three."

Jane was not counting slowly. Caroline's feet moved without a conscious decision from her, carrying her past the two grinning footmen.

"Seven. Eight..."

She began to run, suddenly desperate to get her feet on the stairs, somehow quite certain that if her foot was not on the top step by the time Jane reached ten, that her exit from Netherfield would be more ignominious than she could bear.

"That," the maid Agnes said into the silence left in Caroline's wake, "was the best thing I have *ever* seen."

"Aye, ma'am." Alfred and Andrew were gazing at Jane worshipfully. Betty looked at the door, then at Jane, her brow creased in worry. It was then that Jane noticed the red handprint on the girl's cheek, an exact match to the fingermarks she had seen on Elizabeth's not long ago.

"Betty!" she gasped, stepping forward and reaching to put her hand under Betty's chin gently. "Did Miss Bingley strike you?"

Betty nodded, tears beginning to fall from her reddened eyes. "I should go with her, ma'am," she said anxiously. "Miss Bingley said she'd turn me off without a character."

"No, Betty," Jane dropped her hand from the maid's chin, grasped her hands. "You are employed here at Netherfield, by Mr Bingley and myself, not by Miss Bingley. I assure you that you still have a position, and should you need a character reference, I will write you a glowing one personally."

"I do?" Betty's lower lip trembled.

"If you wish to go with Miss Bingley, I will not prevent it; indeed, I shall think that your loyalty to her is commendable. Should she fail to see to your stipend, I will make sure that it is paid to you." Jane spoke gently, seeing that the girl was distraught. "I have a personal maid already and have no need for another... but my sister Kitty could use a lady's maid, and I should be happy to pay your wages for you to do that duty."

"Oh ma'am," Betty almost choked, and to Jane's horror she slid to her knees and started kissing Jane's hands. "Thank you, ma'am, thank you so much! I'd be right honoured to serve Miss Kitty, that I would! You truly are an angel, ma'am!"

"Oh do get up," Jane hurriedly tugged Betty to her feet, "please, Betty. I promise, you will not be thinking that I am an angel after a few weeks with Kitty!"

Agnes snorted. "After Miss Bingley, serving Miss Kitty will be a cakewalk, ma'am. Betty knows how lucky she is."

"Mind your tongue, Agnes," Mrs Hughes said sharply.

The maid bowed her head penitently before tucking her arm through Betty's. "Come on, Bet," she said bracingly. "Let's go down the servants' stairs, and then you won't even have to see her leave. With your leave, ma'am?"

Jane waved them off, the two footmen following in the maids' wake, before heaving a small sigh. "If only I could escape down the servants' stairs and not have to see her leave either," she murmured to Mrs Hughes.

"You have already defeated the dragon, ma'am. I think you can stand to see her depart in disgrace."

Jane had to bite her lip to keep from smiling at hearing Caroline referred to as a dragon; she gave Mrs Hughes her best stern look, which was apparently completely hopeless because the housekeeper only smiled at her and gave her arm a maternal little pat.

"You were absolutely marvellous, Mrs Bingley. The story will be all over Netherfield within the hour, and I have no doubt the staff will all be utterly devoted to you after you treated Betty so kindly."

"Miss Bingley had slapped her, and I don't doubt that it was not Betty's fault in the slightest. My mother always told me that the true measure of a gentleman, or a lady, is to be found in how they treat their servants. No servant will be mistreated at Netherfield while I am mistress here, you can be very sure of that!" Jane's voice rose a little as she spoke, but it was a subject on which she felt quite passionate.

Descending the stairs with Mrs Hughes a couple of steps behind her, Jane could see through the open front doors that Caroline was already in the carriage, sitting huddled and silent in the corner. Mr and Mrs Hurst were just putting on their hats and gloves ready for departure, Charles bending down to kiss Louisa's cheek before shaking Gerald's hand.

"Take care of Jane, Charles," Louisa told him, laying a hand upon his arm, "and please... enjoy being married. We'll... *manage* Caroline." Seeing Jane descending the stairs, she went to her and embraced her more warmly than she ever had before.

A little surprised, Jane nonetheless returned the embrace, and smiled at Mr Hurst as he made her a deep bow and said gruffly that he looked forward to being in her company again soon.

"Proud to call you family, Mrs Bingley," he said, cheeks an even ruddier shade than usual. "You and *all* your family."

"Since we *are* family, I think you had best call me Jane." Gerald Hurst was no taller than she, so it was easy for her to lay her hand on his arm and salute his cheek with a sisterly kiss. "You and Louisa travel safely, and return to Netherfield soon. Charles and I will be very happy to have you home with us again."

Charles put his arm about her waist and she could almost feel the warmth of his approval as he smiled broadly. "Jane is quite correct, Gerald; we shall always be glad of your company."

Gerald snorted at that, took Louisa's hand upon his arm and turned towards the door. "Then you'd be the first newlywed couple I've met in a while who wanted any company at all beyond each other!"

"Gerald!" Louisa chided as Jane blushed and Charles let out a bellow of laughter. "Really, that might be true but there are some things that are better left unsaid!"

"Don't be missish, Lou. Jane's a married woman now," and Gerald tipped her a wink. Scandalised, Jane found herself blushing and giggling as the Hursts proceeded down the steps and climbed into the carriage; she caught a glimpse of Caroline glaring at her before the footman closed the door and the carriage rumbled away.

The butler closed the front door and slipped discreetly away, leaving Jane and Charles standing alone in the middle of the hall.

There was complete silence for a moment as they listened to the sound of the carriage wheels fading into the distance, and then they looked at each other.

"This is really not quite how I envisioned the first day of our marriage," Charles said dismally.

Jane smiled at him, reaching to put her arms about his neck, careless that anyone could come into the hall and see them. "Is it not? What can I do to improve the day for you, my darling?"

"Jane!" Shocked at the sly innuendo she put behind the words, he gaped down at her. "What have you done with my sweet, innocent Jane?"

"I think it's what *you* did with your sweet, innocent Jane that has caused this," she said with a giggle, before suddenly worrying that he might not care for her more forward behaviour. A frown creased her brow, and she bit down nervously on her lower lip, casting her eyes down.

Charles' arms wrapped around her, pulling her firmly against him. She gasped as she felt a distinct hardness pushing at her through the layers of their clothes.

"I think I like the sensual, knowing Mrs Bingley even more than I liked the sweet, innocent Miss Bennet," he assured her.

"You do?" Jane peeked up at him through her eyelashes.

"Indeed, I believe that I positively *adore* Mrs Bingley," he saw her uncertainty, though he did not understand the cause, and took pains to assure her of his fervent adoration. "And that nothing would make me happier than to retire with her to our chambers for the remainder of the day, to investigate just what ideas she might have to *improve* the day for both of us."

Reassured, Jane's smile returned in full force. "Then let us adjourn upstairs, Mr Bingley. I cannot think of anything else I would rather do."

Catherine Bilson

Always, Mr Bingley

Jane was very glad that she had asked Hannah to dress her in a simple gown, for she did not think that she could have borne taking too long to get undressed. As it was, she and Charles were fumbling at each other's clothes even as he kicked the bedroom door closed behind them. His cravat stubbornly refused to yield, but it actually didn't matter, she realised; she was worrying about the wrong item of clothing, and it was a simple matter for Charles to release the falls of his breeches, toss her skirts up to her waist and hoist her up against the door with his strong hands under her thighs.

"Oh my - oh *Charles*!" she gasped as he entered her with one swift thrust.

"Too much?" he checked, thinking a little late that he should have taken more time to prepare her, that he hadn't exactly been considerate of her comfort. She was warm and wet clasped around him though, her fingers kneading against his shoulders like kitten claws, long lashes drifting down to rest on her alabaster cheeks.

"Not enough," Jane sighed, trying to shift her hips, encourage him to move. Pinned against the door by his weight, though, there was little she could do. "Please, Charles!"

"*Jane*," he groaned her name, seeking her lips with his. She wound her long legs around his waist, rocked herself against him, and he was undone. His thrusts were rough, heedless of her comfort; she did not care in the slightest, kissing him back with equal fervour, urging him to greater efforts until she let out a high wail of pleasure and tightened around him, her face relaxing into the sweetest lines of bliss.

Charles almost sobbed her name again, spurting hotly deep inside her clutching tunnel, pressing his sweaty brow against hers as he sought to catch his breath.

Jane moaned and clung to Charles as he lifted her gently off him and set her on her feet. Her knees would not hold her up, but it seemed that his were distinctly weakened as well. They stumbled to the bed clinging to each other, and toppled to its surface laughing merrily together.

"I feel that I am probably the most scandalous wife who ever lived," Jane said as she fumbled for the laces of her gown, trying to remove it. She felt quite overheated, as though the garment was cooking her alive.

"It would only be scandalous if we behaved so in public, my darling," Charles disagreed, finally pulling his cravat loose and flinging it off the bed. "What happens betwixt husband and wife behind the closed door of their bedroom is none of anyone else's business."

"So, it is not scandalous behaviour if nobody else knows about it?" Jane asked.

"That is a very philosophical question, darling, and one that your poor husband is quite ill-equipped to answer, due to my complete inattention to the subject of philosophy during my studies at Cambridge. You would do better to ask Darcy, only I pray that you find some way to couch your question such that it appears to pertain to another subject entirely than marital relations." Charles finally managed to divest himself of his waistcoat and shirt, throwing them off the bed after his cravat.

Jane dissolved into helpless giggles at the mere idea of asking Darcy about the subject, no matter what terms she managed to couch it in. "He would think that I had run quite mad!"

Grinning, Charles leaned over to help unlace her gown. "Better not ask him then, hm? It shall just have to be one of life's great unanswered mysteries."

Divested of her clothing, Jane curled happily into Charles' arms, resting her cheek on his chest. "It might be all a matter of perspective, too," she mused. "Why, this time yesterday, I would have been utterly shocked at finding myself in this precise situation, and yet now, nothing could seem more natural."

He stroked his hand into her hair, finding the pins which secured it and removing them one by one. "This time yesterday, I felt as though this moment would never come," he confessed. "The day seemed to be going so impossibly slowly."

"Really?" Jane tilted her head to look up at him enquiringly, her hair tumbling loose and drifting in a soft wave of gold across his chest. "The day passed in a terrifying blur for me; it seemed that no sooner was Mama shaking me awake than we were in the church, and then there was the wedding feast..."

"Dare I hope that all of your fears about the marriage bed have been sufficiently assuaged, my darling?" Charles asked when she trailed off into silence.

"Oh yes!" Smiling, she leaned up to kiss him. "More than adequately."

"Excellent." He kissed her back, quite thoroughly, and it was mere moments before he decided that kissing her lips alone was not sufficient for him to express his feelings. Pulling her beneath him, he expressed his adoration of her with kisses to every inch of her skin from her brow to her toes, and back up again.

"I love you," Jane said as he came back to her lips again, and he smiled against her mouth.

"I love you more."

She smiled. She knew this game, or a version of it. "No, I love *you* more," and she dug her fingers into his ribs, wondering even as she did so whether he was actually

153

ticklish. She got her answer when he rolled away yelping with laughter. Jane dived after him, forgetting all about her nakedness. The pair of them rolled around on the bed giggling for several minutes until Charles managed to pin Jane's arms above her head, lying atop her to keep her still.

"You know my deepest, darkest secret now," he said through his laughter, "I can't possibly let you go."

"Were you planning to?"

"Never," he vowed, before kissing her again. "You're mine now, Mrs Bingley."

"Always, Mr Bingley."

~ The End ~

If you enjoyed this book, please do come visit my website at www.catherinebilson.com, where you can find a free printable colouring page I commissioned especially to go with this book!

About The Author

Catherine Bilson was born and raised in North Wales before marrying an Australian and emigrating in 2001. A lifelong fan of Jane Austen, *Mr Bingley's Bride* is her third Austen novel, following the well-received *The Best Of Relations* and *Infamous Relations*.

The Best Of Relations

What if... Aunt Gardiner, who after all hailed from Lambton, was well acquainted with the Darcy family, and knew of Wickham's misdemeanours? How would the story have been different? This tale begins with an exchange of letters between Elizabeth Bennet and her favourite aunt, discussing the happenings in Hertfordshire as the Bennet family become acquainted with their new neighbours, the Bingleys and their house guest Mr Darcy.

Infamous Relations

What if... Mr Collins had been even more despicable than in Jane Austen's original tale? Would such an infamous relation destroy Elizabeth and Darcy's chance of happiness forever, or would his actions set in motion an entirely different sequence of events?

You can catch up with Catherine at her website,
www.catherinebilson.com

or on her Facebook page
fb.me/catherinebilsonauthor

She also writes steamy contemporary romance under the pen name Caitlyn Lynch.